For my dear friend Del whose wonderful banana pudding helped to inspire part of this story

People Smarts

& Wounded Hearts

KC Hart

Paperback ISBN: 978-1-954791-26-8

BOOKS BY KC HART

CHAPTER ONE

*C*allie Madison leaned forward, twirled the red straw through her iced white chocolate mocha latte, and stared across the table at her sister. "It's not like I'm asking you to give me the money. It's a loan. I'll pay it back when I graduate. With interest." She rubbed her lips together, and the sweet chocolate flavor of her coffee mixed with the berry flavor of her lip gloss. "I just don't see what the big deal is. I thought you wanted me to go to college to better myself. I mean, if you think about it, I'm doing this as much for you as I am for myself."

Fiona raised her piping hot black coffee to her lips and blew the swirl of rising steam from the cup. She stared at her younger sister's bouncy blond curls, pulled away from her face with a baby blue headband. The polka dots on the head band matched the blue and white striped tank top that clung to Callie's perfectly toned figure like a well-fitting glove. Her tanned legs, crossed at the knee, emerged from the blue jean mini skirt and continued down to the flashy red toenails showing from the rhinestone studded flip flops. These nails matched the manicured fingernails now drumming the tabletop as her baby sister looked at her, eyes stretched wide. "Cal, this is not easy for me to say, and I think you know it. It's not that we don't want you to have the money. I do want you to finish your education, but it took you three years to finish a two-year junior college. Not because you don't have the brains, because we both know that's not the case. You just started putting other things, like parties and dating and whatever, ahead of studying." Fiona blew out a deep breath of air and took a sip of the coffee. "We're thinking that if you work for a year, save up your money to put toward the tuition, that you will start taking your education seriously."

"You're not being fair." Callie lowered her voice and looked around the Bayou Bean as she leaned back in her chair. A couple of girls she had graduated from junior college with back at the beginning of the summer sat a few tables over near the picture window facing the busy street. Wouldn't they love to know that all the bragging she had done about leaving Carson's Bayou and going to LSU this fall was falling flat on its face? One of the girls, Bridget, the plump one that loved to gossip, looked over her shoulder to where Callie and Fiona sat, the nosy little pigeon. Callie stretched her lips into a broad catlike smile and nodded in Bridget's direction, making sure their eyes met and held. Bridget jerked her head back around, a flush of red climbing up her pigeon neck. Callie turned her gaze back to Fiona. "I had a heavy load with volleyball practice, and then all the debate team meetings. It was too much to keep on top of. Besides, college is supposed to make you a well-rounded person. Part of the reason people go to college is for the social growth experience." Callie batted her eyes at her big sister. "I wasn't doing anything bad, Fi. I just couldn't keep up."

"Hogwash." Fiona set the coffee cup down on the table a little too hard. "Rich people might send their kids to colleges and universities for the social experience, but the rest of us go to learn something that will help us get a decent job and support ourselves for the rest of our lives." Her head cocked to the side, and she glared at her sister. "If you want social growth, go to the library and check out a few books, do a little reading about the world. That will grow you way more than spending all your time with Dawson Wallace. Honestly, Callie, I don't know what you see in that guy."

"There's nothing wrong with Dawson." Callie raised her chin. "He's a sweet guy. He's not a Wade, but I wasn't lucky enough to fall for the richest guy in town." She looked down and rubbed the glossy red surface of the nails on her left hand with the fingers on her right. "You dropped out of college the first time you went." She slowly raised her eyes and looked at Fiona through her thick lashes. "At least I kept going and graduated."

"See?" Fiona spat out the words like they were bad medicine. "That's the reason I'm not letting Langston give you a free ride to LSU. You know good and well that I dropped out to get married. It was stupid and Jeff was a jerk, but while I was there, I did the work and made the grades. I was working hard and saving all I could to go back to school until Nanna got sick." Fiona's words faded away. She reached her hand across the table, the anger vanishing as quickly as it came. Tears glistened in Callie's eyes as Fiona squeezed her hand. "I don't want to fight with you," she said, her voice becoming soft. "I'm not going to fight with you. The fact is, now I have a daughter of my own, and hopefully one day soon, Catherine will have a little brother or sister."

"You're pregnant?" A smile tugged at the corners of Callie's lips; the anger of a few seconds ago completely forgotten.

"Not yet." Fiona returned the smile. "But we're trying."

"Okay." Callie's shoulders slumped forward, and she sniffed back the unshed tears. "What do you want me to do?"

"Don't act like it's the end of the world." Fiona eased her hand back and picked up her mug, the coffee's rich aroma floating up and urging her to continue. A chestnut strand of hair dropped from the pile of messy curls pulled to the back of her head. She brushed it out of the way and sipped her coffee. "Get a job. Save your money. You're living in Sidney's apartment and driving my Beetle. You should be able to save almost every penny if you don't..." Fiona glanced down at Callie's manicured hands. "If you don't let it slip through your fingers. In a year, if you've worked hard and have part of the tuition, we will help you with the rest."

"Is that it? One year of work, and then you help with school?"

"No." Fiona took a bigger sip of the cooling coffee then returned it to the table. "You also have to decide on a major. We won't help pay your tuition if you don't know what you are going to school for. You have an entire year to think about it, so that shouldn't be a problem." Fiona looked down at her cell phone laying on the table. "Oh man, it's already two. I have to pick Catherine up from the sitter." She reached across the table again and squeezed Callie's hand. "Don't be mad at me. I hate it when we are mad at each other."

"I'm not mad." Callie pulled in a deep breath of air and huffed it out. "I'm ready to get through school and get out of this town. Another year stuck in Carson's Bayou is like a prison sentence."

"Well, put on your orange jumpsuit and get to work." Fiona stood from her chair, her gauzy ankle-length skirt draping around her willowy frame. "Your sentence will be over before you know it. There's a HELP WANTED sign over in the window." She nodded her head to the front of the coffee shop where Callie's friends sat. "You can probably

4

start here tomorrow if you don't put me down as a reference."

"I don't know." Callie looked up at her tall, thin, perfect big sister and winked. "Your antics at the Bayou Bean are legendary. I have a feeling simply having the name Madison will forever ban me from employment here.

*N*ope. Callie took out her cell phone and pulled up the help wanted section on the newspaper's website. She might have to work for a year, but she was not going to wait tables or hustle fancy coffee out to her snobby friends. She had an associate degree from the junior college. Yes, it was a general studies degree with the minimal amount of math that she could get away with, but it was still a degree. There had to be something around here she could do besides being a food jockey.

She scrolled past the posting for a cashier at the dollar store and a stocker at the grocery store. She continued through the listing for private sitters for the elderly and daycare workers. "That looks promising." Callie pulled a drink of the sweet coffee concoction through her straw and read the post. *Office manager needed for new business opening August first. Honor Systems Technology is looking for an office manager proficient in planning and organization, analysis and assessment, time management, and communication, multi-tasking and conflict resolution. This person will need to have a thorough understanding of billing clients and running a budget and be proficient in multiple prominent computer software programs.*

The communication thing would not be a problem. Conflict resolution, well she could talk her way out of any problem, especially any dilemma a nerdy computer worker would have to deal with. Callie stuck the tip of her manicured fingernail between her teeth. The rest of the stuff on the list—that was another story.

Crash! Callie jerked her head toward the explosive sound. The barista, a high school girl that probably weighed ninety pounds soaking wet, dropped a tray with a couple of drinks and some pastries, making a soppy sticky mess near the cash register. She turned her head away from the girl and looked over at the help wanted sign in the window of the Bayou Bean. That was the job she was qualified for, but good grief. The two girls she graduated with were laughing, literally laughing out loud at the poor kid near the counter. The hyenas.

Callie got up and hurried to where the girl was kneeling, trying to pick up the mess. "Here," she said, squatting beside her as she picked up the silverware and coffee mugs. "Let me help. Just ignore those biddies. They need to be taught a few manners."

"Thank you." The girl looked at Callie, near hero worship written all over her face. "These trays weigh a ton, and Mr. Randall will have a fit if he hears I spilled one."

Callie helped the poor kid get everything back on the tray, then returned to her table, refusing to look over to the window. She slid into her chair and stared down at the list of requirements for the office manager. She had made a B in creative writing. Her resume might require a little bit of her creative touch, but she needed the office manager's job. Besides, she was twenty-two. She knew as much about computer software as any other likely candidate in Carson's Bayou. The place was not overflowing with technology geeks after all.

Callie pushed her chair back and stood up, stretching her shoulders. She smiled at a couple of guys who looked her way as she headed out the door. She could get this job for sure if the person doing the interview was a dude, but she couldn't bank on that. No, she wouldn't actually lie on her resume, not really. She would be creative. Once she got the position, she would buckle down and figure out everything she needed to know. Fiona said she was smart, and Fiona knew her better than anybody. She could do this. One year of hard work, then bye-bye Carson's Bayou.

CHAPTER TWO

*H*onor Jacobs pulled his ancient green Subaru into the grocery store parking lot and looked around. Some places never changed, and the Carson's Bayou grocery store was one of them. Memories of all the years working at the store as a buggy boy, cashier, janitor, and general flunky strolled through his head. Most of the potholes were missing from the parking lot now, but otherwise, the place was just as he had left it when he turned in his notice his tenth-grade year of high school.

He grabbed his umbrella lying beside him on the cracked leather seat and glanced at his watch. The interviews started in an hour. He had plenty of time to run in and get a sandwich and a bottle of water, then drop by his house to grab a shower before heading to the office. A change of clothes was definitely required. His running shorts and tee-shirt with the arms ripped out didn't scream respectable business owner.

Honor slammed the car door, and it let out its usual arthritic squeak. He glanced up at a gray, angry looking cloud pushing in front of the sun. Yeah, rain was definitely on the way. He could smell it in the air. A gust of wind blew an empty food bag across the pavement and under a nearby truck.

"Now y'all be good inside." Honor turned toward the gravelly voice a couple of vehicles away. "Don't whine for stuff you know we can't get, and I'll make us some chocolate pudding tonight after supper."

Honor watched the man, probably in his early thirties, dressed in faded jeans, ancient cowboy boots, and a wrinkled tee-shirt, herding two young kids who looked to be about three and four between the vehicles. A curly-headed toddler perched on his hip with her thumb securely stuck in her mouth. They all looked clean and cared for, but their stretched and faded clothes had seen better days.

"Daddy," the oldest child, and the only boy, took hurried steps to keep up with his father's long legs. "I want ice cream."

"I'll put the pudding in the fridge and let it get really cold so it will taste like ice cream." The father looked down at his son, then back at the little girl lagging behind her brother. "We can't lose you, little bug. I better tote you too." He squatted down and scooped the girl up in one fluid motion and landed her on his other hip. "One day soon we will have ice cream, the three flavors kind, so you can have strawberry and chocolate together in the same bowl like you like it."

Honor followed a few feet behind the family through the sliding glass doors and into the cool air-conditioned store. He smiled at the tired-looking man as he plopped all three children into the buggy. A grocery store version of "Georgia On My Mind", complete with violins, flutes and oboes, floated through the air around them.

The family went in one direction, and Honor in another, heading toward the deli to grab his sandwich. Once he got set up at work and at his house, he would fix his lunch every day, not wasting money, but today he would have to splurge on the store made food. He grabbed the turkey and sharp cheddar on whole wheat in the see-through plastic box and picked up a granny smith apple from the produce on the way toward the checkout. He picked up a bottle of water but put it back. He probably still had enough ice water in his thermos for lunch.

Honor glanced up and down the rows of check-out lines and walked to the one on the opposite end of the store near the front desk. A round, balding man in a canvas vest with a smile on his face waited for him to step forward. "There's a man coming to check out in a few minutes," Honor said, laying the sandwich and shiny green apple on the black conveyor line. The food crept the couple of feet forward toward the happy cashier. "He has three little children, a boy and two girls. The guy has on a blue tee-shirt with Willie Nelson on the back."

"That's Drake Lewis and his kids. I saw them come in right in front of you." The food tumbled forward onto the silver checking area in front of the cashier. He pushed a button, stopping the conveyor. "He comes in every couple of days and buys a few things, always has the kids with him. He's got his hands full. His wife had some kind of illness. She died just a couple of months after the littlest girl was born."

"Could you do me a small favor?" The corners of Honor's lips turned up into a small, tight smile, listening to the cashier, but not encouraging further comments. "Run him a five-hundred-dollar tab." He stuck his debit card in the machine in front of the checking area. "Add it to my sandwich, and I'll pay for it now, but don't tell him where the money came from."

"Like a gift certificate?" The cashier's fingers stopped running the sandwich over the scanner, and he stared at Honor.

"Yeah. That'll work, as long as it's anonymous."

The cashier's eyebrows pulled together as he looked at Honor. "Let me get the manager," he finally said, a toothy grin breaking out across his face.

"Just hurry, okay?" Honor glanced over his shoulder. The man and his kids weren't in any of the checkout lines yet. "I have to be somewhere soon, and it looks like the bottom is fixing to fall out of the sky any minute."

"That about figures." Giant drops of icy bone chilling rain poured down onto Callie's head as she started across the grocery store parking lot. She glanced back at her car, but it was just as far away now as the store's sliding glass doors several yards in front of her. She should have pulled into the fire lane like she usually did to run in and grab a plate lunch, but Kenny, the store manager, had asked her to stop doing that last Friday when she came in. She'd been parking in that fire lane for years. Why was he getting in such a huff now? Nobody had ever died or anything from her being there for the fifteen minutes it took her to run in and out of the store. If she didn't love their chicken and dumplings so much, she would stop giving the store her business.

A gust of wind lifted a soggy sales paper up from a nearby buggy someone had left in a parking space. It slapped it against her powder pink satin blouse. "No, no, no." Cassie let out a low moan and pulled the soppy paper, advertising chicken breasts ninety-nine cents a pound and string beans two cans for a dollar, from her chest. She didn't have time for this. She had written the perfect resume last night on her laptop. She still had to run by the Wade office and get Lucas or Langston to print off a copy for her interview. They had that nice, thick paper they used for special documents that would surely make the right impression on the person she had to talk to.

Fiona had actually suggested she print off the resume at her husband's business when they talked earlier in the week. She was thrilled that Callie was trying to get the job, and even told her to use Langston as a reference, since she had worked filing at his office for a few weeks last summer. Of course, Fiona would have a conniption fit if she saw the padded resume. That's why she waited until the last minute to print it today, while Fiona was at the library with Catherine doing toddler story time.

Callie tilted her head down, looking like a drowned rat, pushing against the wind and rain now coming down in sheets. How could she possibly go to the interview looking like this? The satin blouse clung to her body like a slimy second skin. At least the knit skirt was black, and she wouldn't look like she had wet herself. A bolt of lightning sliced across the sky, followed by a growling rumble of thunder. Callie broke into a run, splashing her cute nude sandals through the water running into the drainage grate near the buggy return.

Callie's down-turned head and shoulders slammed into the man's unmoving chest like a gnat bouncing off a brick wall. "What the!" Her sandals skidded on the slippery wet pavement, and her backside propelled backwards, her feet sliding forward. She flailed out her arms, waving in the air for something, anything, to stop her fall. An arm, a tanned muscular arm, reached down like an anchor through the storm. She grabbed the arm and latched on like her life depended on it, trying to find her footing in the watery mess below. The man, the same man who had knocked her backwards in the first place, lifted her back up, her backside an inch from the nasty drainage grate below.

She glared down at her clothes, her mud streaked legs and her soggy shoes, as she continued to hold on to the man's arm. Her jaw clenched, and she slung her head back. Soppy blond hair, now matted with drenched hair products, flew backwards out of her face. How dare this guy run into her like that? She jerked her hand away from his grip and cut icy blue eyes up to the man standing in the shadow of his umbrella. "What do you think you're doing mowing people down like that in the grocery store parking lot?" She shouted over the sound of the pelting rain. "What if I'd been a little old lady? You would have just broken my hip. I ought to sue you."

The beast grabbed her arm again and drug her under the umbrella with him, pulling her along to the dryness of the storefront's covered walkway.

"Stop it, you!" Callie wrestled against the man's grip on her arm, and he finally let her go. She looked down again at her clothes. Well, there went that job. Maybe she could call and reschedule, tell them she had a flat or rescued an injured puppy or something, and would be a few minutes late.

"Oatmeal? Is that you?"

Callie's head snapped up and glared at the man, the man who mowed over innocent women in torrential weather. He pulled the umbrella away from his head and lowered it to the ground. The man pushed black hair away from his forehead, and a pair of familiar green eyes stared down at Callie. "Duck Jacobs, I'm going to kill you."

CHAPTER THREE

*H*onor stared down at the woman in front of him, his brow furrowed. Yes, it was definitely Callie Madison, but a mature, womanly, mad as a wet hen version of the girl he remembered from his childhood. The last time he had seen or spoken to her was the day he left school. He had been a sophomore, and she an eighth-grader.

"Will you still eat lunch with me next year, Duck?" Callie had asked, closing the now empty thermos of her daily lunch of oatmeal. "I'll be in high school too, but I know it's not super cool for juniors to sit with freshmen."

"When have I ever been super cool?" He had finished his cheeseburger and fries and was opening the little vanilla ice cream container. "Besides, I don't sit with you. You come over here and sit with me, remember?"

"That's true." She had winked in her usual joking and take-charge kind of way. "Matter of fact, it will probably help your social status immensely to be seen with me."

The bell blared. Her enormous blue eyes, made even bigger by mascara and eyeliner she hid in her purse and applied every morning in the junior high bathroom, sparkled. She had hustled away, her blond hair pulled back in a ponytail swinging right to left with every step.

Honor blinked away the memory and looked at the woman in front of him. Black smudges circled her eyes. This and the soppy wetness of her clothes and hair kind of gave her a walking dead vibe, but she was still Callie Madison in all her glory, still attracting attention and chaos wherever she went.

"It is Duck, isn't it?" Callie stared up at him, her cheeks puffed out, blowing rivers of rain from her eyes. "You've changed—a lot, but I recognize you. You almost knocked me down, Duck." Callie turned her head down to her soaked shirt and pulled the front away from her skin, tugging against the wet fabric suctioned to her flat abdomen. "And look at me. I'll never make it to my interview on time now." She glared back up at him, her eyes demanding an answer.

"Hold on, Oatmeal."

"Callie. Nobody ever called me Oatmeal but you, and it was always so embarrassing."

"Okay, Callie." The corner of Honor's mouth pushed up in a lopsided grin. Yes, this was definitely the girl from his past. That attitude was one of a kind. "I didn't knock you down. I rescued you. You bulldozed into me, and I saved you from falling on that drainage grate."

"You did not." Callie's hands went to her hips, her jaw clenched. "I was walking across the parking lot like a normal person, and you rammed me down."

"You were running across the parking lot with your head down and ran into me." Honor's voice took on a patronizing tone. "We can ask the people inside or look at the security videos if you want, but that is how it happened." Unless the grocery store had done a huge upgrade in the years he'd been gone, the cameras in the parking lot were not connected to anything and were there for show. Even so, somebody inside probably saw what happened.

"Well." Callie rolled her eyes and tugged on her drenched black skirt. "Either way, now I'm a hot mess, and I'll never get that job. I guess I'll call and cancel or just not show up."

"Or go in and tell them what happened." Honor shrugged his shoulders. "People get wet in the rain all the time and can still do their jobs. The Oatmeal I remember would never throw in the towel that easily."

"I could sure use a towel." Callie pulled a dripping wet strand of hair from the side of her face and tucked it into the sodden mass of curls. "When did you get into town? You left me back in school without saying goodbye, and now you've come back without saying hello. I thought we used to be friends, Duck."

"We were." Honor's lips turned down as he remembered his last day in Carson's Bayou all those years ago. "I didn't have much choice in how I left. Mom dropped a bomb on Dad about leaving him. He gave me two hours to pack and be in the car. We stopped by and withdrew me from school, and I ran into the grocery store and quit, then we hit the road." Honor looked down at Callie's face, staring up at him, the anger in her eyes melting away. "But you're right. I could have called, at least."

"I knew your mom and dad split, but wow. That was kind of brutal." Callie put a hand on her hip, and her eyes traveled up and down Honor's ancient running shoes, baggy gym shorts, and tee-shirt with the torn-out arm holes. "What are you doing back? Are you the new high school football coach or something? That would be a hoot. Duck Jacobs, former dumpy high school nerd, now ordering around all the kids of his old jock classmates. You could really get payback from a few of those guys if you were a mind, too."

Honor ran his hand through the top of his wavy black

hair, glancing down at his clothes. "No, no coaching for me. I just finished a run in the park, but that would be ironic. I stopped by here for a sandwich." He held up the plastic grocery bag in his hand. "I'm headed home to change, then going to work." He glanced across the parking lot. The rain had stopped just as quickly as it started. The sun peaked out from behind a few clouds. "Look. I think the weather is clearing up. At least you won't have to run through the rain to get back to your car."

"A lot of good that will do me. I'm never getting that job now, but like you said, what have I got to lose? I might as well go and try, even if I look like a drowned poodle."

"Might as well." A grin broke out across Honor's face. "It was nice seeing you, Oat—I mean Callie. Maybe when I get settled in, we can get together and talk about old times. Do you still live with your Nana?"

"No, she passed away a few years ago. Sidney got married and lives in our old house with his wife and daughter. They redid the place, and it's pretty nice. I live in an apartment over his garage by the old garment factory."

"I'm sorry to hear about your Nana. She was a nice lady." Honor glanced toward the side of town Callie was talking about. "I know where that garage is. I wondered who ran the place. Good for Sid. Sounds like he's doing alright."

"He is, and so is Fi." Callie pulled in a deep breath and blew it out through puffed cheeks. "Speaking of doing good, I better get a move on. If I am going to go to that interview, I better hustle up. I still have to run and print my resume."

"What about going in the store?"

"I was running in to grab a plate of chicken and dumplings for lunch. They're my favorite. Mrs. Helga in the deli makes them about as close to Nana's as I can find." Callie rubbed a drop of water from her nose. "But I don't have time now, and I've kind of lost my appetite. I'll just grab something later." She tilted her head up and smiled. "It was good seeing you, Duck. I'm glad you're back in town."

"Same to you, Oatmeal."

"You really can't keep calling me that." Callie ran her finger under her eye, smearing the black line of mascara even more. "I never understood why you insisted on calling me Oatmeal anyway. I brought it to school for lunch a lot, but not every single day."

"You brought it every single day that I remember," Honor said, snorting out a laugh. "That's not the real reason I called you Oatmeal."

"Well, enlighten me." Callie raised her eyebrows. "What was the real reason?"

"It was because you got all mushy every time you saw me."

Callie stared at her reflection in the little mirror of her compact. Not a lick of makeup on, and her hair was scraped back in a tight ponytail. At least she didn't look like a zombie cartoon character anymore with makeup smeared from can to can't. She had tidied up in the bathroom at the Wade offices as best she could while the secretary made a couple of copies of her resume. Her pink shirt was damp and wrinkled, and the moist skirt felt awful against her skin, but she had wiped the mud splatter from her legs. She would explain what happened. Some careless guy had run into her during the sudden storm, and she didn't have time to change. There was probably zero hope of getting the job looking as mousy as she looked. At least the resume was sort of impressive, with Langston Wade as a reference. Everyone in town knew him, so Duck was right. Might as well go in and try.

She got out of the Beetle and stood, looking up and down the sidewalk. She could have walked the short distance from the Wade building to this address, just a block down, but the way her day was going, a tornado would have blown her and her beautiful resume to kingdom come.

She walked up the sidewalk past the new little pizza place that opened up during the spring and paused in front of a small storefront. At one time, back when she was a kid, this place had been a mom and pop shoe store. It had shut down years and years ago. As far as she could remember, the little building had remained vacant since that time. Like so many other places on this side of town now, someone was revamping the old and starting something new.

Callie stared at Honor System Enterprises, painted on the glass in white letters in a stiff, business like font. She pulled in a slow, deep breath and opened the door. An electronic doorbell dinged as she stepped inside, and a waft of glacier like air hit her damp hair and clothes.

"Hello." Callie walked up to the man, probably around her age, maybe a little older, with horn-rimmed glasses and a gray plaid shirt. "I'm Callie Madison. I have a two o'clock interview."

The man tapped the computer screen on his desk, then looked up with a polite smile. "He's expecting you. Go through those doors."

The heels of Callie's sandals clicked across the hardwood floor, and she could feel the goosebumps popping out on her legs. Great, might as well complete the mousy, country hick girl look. She opened the door and stepped into the little office with plain white sheetrock walls, not a single picture or adornment in sight, a far cry from the Wade offices. She looked across the immaculately neat desk to a man's back as he stared out the window. His shoulders and the back of his head looked familiar. "Excuse me." She stepped forward to where a chair set on her side of the desk. "I'm Callie Madison. I'm here about the office manager position."

"Aren't you glad you came on in?" Duck Jacobs turned and grinned at Callie, like the cat that swallowed the canary.

"Did you know this was where I was going?" Callie gulped back the anger rising in her throat. "Is that why you told me to go on to the interview? So you could make fun of me?" She felt her skin turning red, probably a beautiful sight with her slicked back hair and no makeup face. "That's low, Duck." She swallowed the lump of emotions. Her eyes darted around the room, then settled on his face. "You should give me the job just to prove that you aren't as big a jerk as you are appearing to be."

Laughter exploded from Duck's chest, and he waved his arm toward the chair. "No, I did not know you were coming in for the position until I got here. You should know me better than that." He eased into the plain looking computer chair behind the desk and grinned. His laughter dying down to a soft chuckle. "Besides, I figured you knew it was me and were playing one of your games."

"What games?" Callie passed her resume across the desk to Duck, her jaw set in a firm line. "And how would I know you were the guy running this place? I'm not a mind reader."

"Callie." Duck raised one eyebrow. "The business is Honor Systems. My name is Honor. Connect the dots."

"Your name is Caleb Jacobs," Callie said, her eyes shooting darts across the desk. She should be smooching up, trying to get the job, but Duck always knew how to push her buttons. "I should know. All the teachers ever talked about was Caleb Jacobs this or Caleb Jacobs that. Geesh, Duck. You had every teacher at that school wrapped around your finger."

"Not the coaches." Duck opened the pale blue Manilla

folder and looked down at the resume. "Honor is my middle name. It's what my parents called me. The school always insisted I go by my first name. I tried to get them to call me Honor up to the third grade, then I quit bucking the system." He looked from the papers to Callie. "You knew my name was Honor. I've told you that before."

"I guess so." Callie bit her lower lip. "Sorry." Time to eat a little crow. She really needed this job, and letting her temper get away from her was not the way to get it. "You're right. I forgot." She put a smile on her face and looked across the desk. "I don't guess there's any reason to explain why I look like a drowned rat."

"No." Duck flipped to the second page of the papers. "But you need to explain this ridiculous resume."

CHAPTER FOUR

"*R*eally, Callie. Extensive experience in computer logistics." Honor glanced up from the paper, one eyebrow raised. "Is that true?"

"Yes." Callie's eyes darted from Honor's face to the blank wall on his left. She pulled her lower lip in with her teeth. "I'm extremely proficient in using algorithms, too." Her eyes narrowed, and she pushed her lips out into a pout. "Oh, good grief, Duck. You weren't supposed to actually look at all that stuff. I was going to be sweet and charming and..."

"And schmooze your way into this job." Honor's face broke into a telling grin as his eyes traveled up and down the expensive looking paper filled with fiction. "It probably would have worked too, but I happen to know you a little too well for that."

"And that is so not fair." Callie plopped down in her chair and tugged her skirt down into place. "I promise, Duck, if you will give me a chance, I can learn everything I need to learn. I know I can do this job."

"Do you even know what computer logistics is?" Honor

glanced down at the rest of the fairy tale on the paper and closed the folder. "Is any of what's in here true?"

"I googled it." Callie rolled her lips together and twisted her hips in the chair. "A lot of what's on there is true. It's not like I'm a liar. I graduated from college this past spring, and I worked summers at Wade Enterprises."

"Wade Enterprises?" Honor leaned back in the chair enjoying the view. "You know, I could always tell when you were lying. You have a tell."

"I'm not lying." Callie glared across the desk, her eyes shooting sparks. "What tell?"

"I think I'll keep that little bit of information to myself." The corners of Honor's eyes crinkled. He hadn't had this much fun in a long time, certainly not since he had broken up with Sheila. "What did Google have to say about computer logistics? I'm dying to know."

"Oh hush," Callie snapped. "Don't be a know it all, Duck. That's just plain rude."

"Look, Callie, this isn't me helping you with your algebra like when we were kids. This is my business. I need someone in this position who will not only represent my product, but will also represent me as a business owner to the people here in town."

"I can do it, Duck. I mean, Caleb, or, Honor, or whatever you want me to call you." Callie ran her fingertips across her forehead. "You know I'm a quick learner. You remember how you would help me cram for those algebra exams? I always passed them when you explained the equations to me." She scooted to the edge of the chair. "Please, Duck. At least consider me. I promise I won't let you down." Callie shoved her hand into her purse, her eyes stretched wide as "Start Me Up", a suddenly obvious poor choice in a ring tone, no matter how much she liked the Rolling Stones, blared from her cell phone. "Sorry."

"I don't know, Callie." Honor watched her fumble with her phone, turning off the ringer, and dropping it back in her bag. "I really don't think you are the person for this job."

"You know this is not how this interview was supposed to go." Callie blinked her eyes and raised her chin. "You know I'm not at my best right now, and you know why. The least you could do is call me back for a second interview and let me prove myself."

Honor drummed his fingertips together, staring at the woman across the desk. "Okay," he finally said, eyebrows drawn low over his murky green eyes. "Come back tomorrow, and we'll do this again."

"You're not going to regret this, Duck." Callie's face lit up with relief. "Tomorrow you will see the real me, and you are going to be impressed."

"Speaking of the real you." Honor handed the blue folder back to Callie as he stood. "If you want me to consider hiring you, go home and redo your resume. Take out all the fiction, and bring me back the facts."

"It won't have a lot on it." Callie frowned.

"I don't care." Honor stepped around the desk and opened the office door. "If you want this job, and I'm not saying I will hire you, but if you want to work for me, you have to be honest. There will be no talking out of both sides of your mouth."

"Just keep an open mind. Okay, Duck?" Callie stood from her chair and slipped her purse onto her shoulder. "Remember that a person is a lot more than what is said about them on a resume."

Honor followed Callie through the front office and watched as she headed down the street to get in the beat-up old Volkswagen Beetle. She climbed in the car and pulled out onto the street, disappearing from sight with the cell phone to her ear, and a stern look of determination on her face.

"Are you going to hire her?"

Honor turned and looked at Clutch, his best friend and business partner. "Don't be crazy. She is probably the least qualified person in Carson's Bayou to fill the position." He strolled back over to where Clutch sat behind his desk. "That's the girl I ran into this afternoon."

"The one that got soaked at the grocery store?" Clutch let out a low whistle. "If she looks like that after being drowned in a rainstorm, I sure would like to see her when she was all cleaned up."

"Well, you'll get your chance. She's coming in for another interview tomorrow."

"I thought you just said she's not qualified for the job." Clutch crossed his arms over his chest and leaned back in his chair. "Why are you bringing her back in?"

"I've got an idea." Honor sat on the edge of the desk and pulled a pen from a cup near his leg. "You are going to be here for six months. Between you and me, we don't really need an office manager. I mean, who is going to be managed? There's just the two of us." He twirled the pen between his fingers and looked down at his friend. "What we really need is someone to help us with the PR. Someone who can talk to these school board members and principals about the educational software, and the administrators and office managers and whatever for the health systems software."

"You're right about that." Clutch sat forward in the chair. "I break out in hives when I try to attend one of those meetings. You do okay with the tech stuff, but let's face it. You are good at explaining the technical aspects of what we do, but we need someone to explain to these people the practical applications of why they need our software."

"Exactly." Honor nodded. "Callie is sharp. I am sure I can teach her how our software will help the teachers organize their subjects and put the information in a format for the different levels of learning needed for their kids. Once she understands how it works, she will be great at selling it to the school systems." He hopped up from the corner of the desk and pointed his finger down at Clutch. "This is going to work out great. If Callie is half of the talker that I remember, she will be perfect for this."

"What about running the office?"

"I'll teach her what she needs to know around here before you pull out and go back to our Houston branch in six months." Honor looked out the large plate-glass window across the front of the building. "She's a local girl with plenty of brains and a lot of spunk. She doesn't know beans about computer software, but neither do the people we are selling it to. She can become our go between."

"She's also easy on the eye." Clutch watched Honor pace back and forth in front of his desk. "Are you sure there wasn't ever anything between you two?"

"No." Honor stopped pacing and laughed. "I left Carson's Bayou when she was in junior high, but even if we had been older, it wouldn't have mattered. I was a pudgy geek that played video games and tutored math. She was way out of my league."

"But not anymore." Clutch studied his friend. "You haven't been on a single date since your breakup with Sheila. This girl might be just the person to bring you back into the land of the living."

"Not hardly." Honor dropped the ink pen back into the cup on the desk and stepped over to his office door. "When I decide to start dating again, I won't be going out with anyone like Callie Madison. That's for sure. If there was any thought of that in my head, the last thing I would do would be to hire her to work here."

Honor went back into his office and closed the door.

Clutch was one of the smartest IT guys he had ever met, but when it came to relationships, he was totally clueless.

Honor was over Sheila, finally over Sheila. She had about destroyed him when she broke off their engagement last year. He thought they had been perfect for each other. They were both homebodies, both a little boring, both no nonsense, practical sorts. When she gave him back the ring and said she needed more than he could give, he didn't understand what she meant. Not until she moved to Florida and married a scuba instructor she had met online.

No, he was over Sheila, but now was not the time for romance. He wanted to put down some roots in the town he considered his home, make a name for himself, build his business and his life here. Maybe then he would find a woman who wanted the same things he wanted. When the time came, he would find someone who wanted to live a nice quiet life in a nice quiet town. Someone he could trust. Callie's bright blue eyes shooting sparks of anger and ringed with smudged black eyeliner flashed through his mind. A lopsided grin spread across his face. No, no danger of Callie Madison ever being girlfriend material. That was for sure.

CHAPTER FIVE

"*I* smell barbecue." Callie dropped her purse on the leather sofa and hurried through Fiona's enormous living room into the kitchen, swanky enough to be on one of those cooking shows her sister loved to watch. "Where's Catherine?"

"She's upstairs napping." Fiona dipped an enormous spoonful of pickle relish into the silver bowl full of potato salad makings. "We went for a swim until she got tired, then I put her down for the afternoon so I could finish supper. Did you bring the watermelon?"

"Oh man. I forgot we were all coming here for supper." Callie slid onto the barstool and glanced at the baby monitor sitting on the counter. "We won't wake her up with our talking, will we?"

"No, she can't hear us." Fiona stirred the relish into the potato salad and dipped out a teaspoonful and passed it across the counter. "How's that? Need more relish?"

"No, but it needs more salt, pepper, and mustard." Callie pulled her cell phone out of the back of her jeans shorts pocket. "I'm gonna text Sid and tell him to get a watermelon."

"Langston doesn't like a lot of mustard." Fiona pulled another teaspoon out of a drawer and dipped out a bite of the salad. "You're right though. It definitely needs salt and pepper." She picked Callie's spoon up from where it lay on the counter and put both spoons in the sink behind her. "Where have you been all day? Did you get that job at the Bayou Bean? Did you apply at that other place you were talking about? I wouldn't get my hopes up about that one."

"No to Bayou Bean." Callie's lips curled into a smile. "I never applied." She propped both elbows on the counter and waited for her sister's reaction.

"I thought you said you were going to follow the plan." Fiona jerked the handle on the pepper mill. "We're serious, Cal. No job, no tuition."

"I'll have you know that I have a job." Callie leaned back from the bar and looked down at her manicured nails, ignoring her sister's glare.

"Where? The snow cone stand? If you are going to work there and have it count, you have to work more than ten hours a week."

"No, not the snow cone stand either."

"Well?" Fiona set down the pepper mill and stared at Callie. "Quit stringing me along. Where are you working?"

"Do you remember Caleb Jacobs? The pudgy guy in your class who always helped me with my pre-algebra?"

"Yeah." Fiona picked up the saltshaker and shook some into the potato salad. "Why? Is this that other job you were talking about?"

"It sure is. He's moved back to Carson's Bayou and is opening up some kind of computer business called Honor Systems Technology."

"Honor Systems. Cute." Fiona set down the saltshaker and began stirring the potato salad again. "He tried to get every-body to call him Honor when we were little, but the teacher insisted he use his first name." Fiona tapped her chin with her pointer finger and looked at the bowl. "Grab me a purple onion from the fridge. He gave you a job?"

"I go back for my second interview tomorrow, but I'm sure he's going to hire me." Callie slid off the barstool and retrieved a purple onion from the enormous stainless-steel refrigerator. "You aren't going to ruin the potato salad with onion, are you?"

"No, I'm not, but I am going to add some to it. It's too bland right now." Fiona took the onion from Callie's hand and pulled a wooden cutting board from the cabinet below the bar. "It needs a little kick."

"Well, dip me out a little and put it to the side. I will kick mine with mustard, like normal people do."

"What are you going to be doing at Honor Systems?" Fiona pulled a knife from a drawer and began chopping the onion. "Don't forget to get the watermelon."

"I'm not sure. Some kind of office manager." Callie looked at her phone laying on the counter and read the text. "Sid said he will bring the watermelon. You probably wouldn't recognize Duck now. He's not pudgy anymore. He's actually kind of cute."

"Really?" Fiona looked up from the onion, her eyes starting to water from the smell. "I can't imagine that. He was such a quiet, geeky guy back before he left. You know his mother ended up leaving town with that semi-pro ballplayer not long after Caleb and his father moved away. What was that guy's name?"

"I don't know. I don't remember any of that stuff. I just know Duck was here one day and gone the next. He hurt my feelings."

"I forgot that you two were friends. He never did really hang out with the other kids in our class. Why did you call him Duck, anyway?"

"Because he was always calling me Oatmeal, and I needed a name for him. One of his favorite things to tell me was that if I didn't get my ducks in a row that I wouldn't get a scholarship for college. I told him he would have to be my duck because I wasn't going to make it through algebra without him tutoring me." Callie's voice softened. "I haven't thought about that in a long time. He was my Duck."

"Sounds like you were a little sweet on him."

"Ewe." Callie curled her upper lip. "Sweet on Duck? No way. He was like another brother or something."

"Are you sure?" Fiona wiped a tear from her cheek with the back of her hand. "You just said that he's cute." She sniffed and looked at the pile of onions on the chopping board. "That's gonna have to be enough. These things are making me squall like a baby."

"Just because he's cute now doesn't mean he's any less nerdy than he was back in school." Callie paused and listened as Catherine's cry floated from the baby monitor. "You want me to go check on her?"

"No. I'll go. You can finish the potato salad though."

Callie stepped around the counter as Fiona disappeared out of the kitchen. Her brow wrinkled as she stared down at the pile of neatly chopped purple onion. She hurried into the pantry and returned with an empty dollar store bag. Onions did not go in potato salad. Everybody would thank her later. She slid the plastic bag over the cutting board and dumped the potent pile of onions in. Her nostrils flared as she pulled out the empty wooden board and stuck it in the sink, then tied up the fragrant bag and dropped it in the trash.

She pulled the mustard from the fridge and squirted a generous loop into the enormous bowl of potato salad. Langston wouldn't care. He probably wouldn't even notice. She quickly stirred the mustard in and ran her finger through the center. Her brow wrinkled. It still wasn't right.

She sprinkled in a little more salt and pepper, stirred it again, and dipped her finger through the concoction a second time. Perfect. She covered the bowl with plastic wrap and slid it into the refrigerator. She looked at the shelves of juices, lunch meats, raw vegetables, and containers of leftovers. Supper was still a few hours away, and she was hungry. She finally pulled a peach from the crisper and shut the door.

"You finish the potato salad?" Fiona stepped into the kitchen with a sleepy-looking Catherine on her hip. "I'm going to fix us a drink, and we are going out back to the swing."

"The potato salad is good to go and waiting in the fridge." Callie stepped over to the sink and rinsed off the peach. "I guess I'll head home for a while. I have to tighten up a few things on my resume before I go back for my next interview tomorrow."

"Start Me Up" floated up from Callie's hip pocket. Fiona frowned as her sister silence her phone. "Are you dating Dawson Wallace again? You know he's nothing but trouble."

"We aren't dating." Callie's eyes narrowed as she ripped a paper towel from the roll near the sink. "I've got to go. I'll be back later."

Callie strode from the kitchen and snatched her purse from the couch on the way out the front door. That was the second time Dawson had tried calling her today. She tossed her purse into the car and slid behind the wheel. Even though she had left the windows in the vehicle down, there were still heat devils darting from the dash. She started the car and headed down the driveway to the road, shifting into second with her fingertips. She would not talk to Dawson. If she talked to him, he would tell her another sad story, explain why he needed her in his life, tell her that the drinking had stopped, that he had been wrong about the baby.

Callie hit the brakes at the bottom of the hill and swallowed back the ache that pushed up along with the memory. Stupid, stupid, stupid. She should never have gotten involved with Dawson, should never have believed him when he said he loved her. She should never have slept with him, given him the one and only part of her that was completely hers to give. If only she could take it all back, be strong like Fiona, or wise like Sydney.

"I think I'm pregnant." Callie would never forget that morning. "I'm two months late, Dawson. I'm scared."

"Don't worry. This happened with Lou and his girlfriend last year." Dawson had not even batted an eye, kept right on shooting his basketball while he talked. "I'll get the name of the doctor they used, and we will get this problem taken care of."

She had not taken care of their baby—the problem, as Dawson suggested. She ignored the knot in her throat that formed every time her mind drug her back to that day. Her periods had started back—no baby, but things had changed. She had changed. She had spent all that time following Dawson Wallace around like a lovesick puppy, blowing off volleyball practice until they kicked her off the team, coming in late, not studying, almost flunking out of school. What had it gotten her? A long look in the mirror that morning told her one thing. She was a stupid college girl that had nearly blown her one hope of bettering herself for a guy that looked at her as nothing more than a good time, at their baby as a problem.

After that, she buckled down and finished the semester without any more partying. She broke it off with Dawson, leaving him and everything he now represented to her. The next semester, much to Fiona's happiness, she took several extra classes and finally finished up junior college.

Why in the world would Dawson Wallace be calling her

now? She wasn't angry at him anymore. He had asked, and she had given. She was the idiot in the picture. He was not a bad guy, really. He had not forced her to do anything she had not agreed to. If anything, he made her see how stupid she had been. The baby. Had there been a baby? Had her not wanting the baby caused her to lose the baby? That was the one thing she could never forget, at least not as long as she was in Carson's Bayou. Not where she was surrounded by the constant reminders of what she was, what she had done.

Callie pulled her phone out of her purse and pulled up Dawson's number. "Blocked." She punched the button and tossed the phone on the passenger's seat. "No more Dawson, no more men, period. It's time to get real with my life." She pulled out of the drive and shifted the car from first to second. She would be blatantly honest on her resume and dare Caleb Honor Jacobs to not give her the job. She would make it through this year, figure out a major, and start a new life in a new town, free of all the dumb mistakes she made in Carson's Bayou. A clean slate and a new life—just make it through the year.

CHAPTER SIX

$\mathcal{C}$allie handed the single sheet of paper across the desk to Duck. "I know it doesn't look like much. I promise though, if you will give me a chance, just a month, I'll prove to you that I can run this office better than any of your other applicants."

"Take a seat, Callie." Honor took the paper from her hand and sat in his chair. "Clutch and I talked yesterday after you left. We decided we really don't need an office manager."

"But." Callie's shoulders stiffened as she stared across the desk. "Duck, you haven't even given me a chance."

"Listen to me before you fly off the handle. I still want you to come to work for me, for us, but in a different position. How do you feel about marketing?"

"Marketing?" Callie's brow softened, and she relaxed against the back of the chair. "Like telling people about whatever it is you do here and convincing them they need some of it?"

"Sort of." Honor glanced at the resume in his hand and laid it on the desk. "This office is going to be a satellite office, but our main office will continue to be in Houston. All the billing and bookkeeping can continue to go through that office. What we want you to do is to learn how to use our software from a..." Honor pressed his lips together, searching for the right word. "From a non-technical point of view. Then, you can help me talk to our clients and explain in lay terms what our products can do for them."

"So, you want me to translate geek-speak into something the average person can understand?"

"I wouldn't call it geek-speak, but yeah. That's the general idea."

"How about nerd-word?" Callie's eyes twinkled. "Is that better?"

"No." Honor smiled, flashing a perfect set of white teeth helped along by four years of braces during high school. "I think geek-speak might be the better choice. Is this job something you would be interested in pursuing?"

"Hmm." Callie raked her teeth across her lower lip and cut her eyes to the left, away from Duck's smiling face. She didn't need to look too eager, too desperate for the job. "Tell me a little more about what I will be required to do," she said, looking back, the joking smile gone from her face.

"Clutch and I will teach you all about the educational software. That's the product we want you to start with. You will go through the training program we developed for teachers, school counselors, and other educators. Once you are familiar with it from that end, we will go over the cost effectiveness of using it and all the data and statistics that support how it improves learning outcomes."

"You're going to pay me to come in every day and go to school?" Callie shifted in her chair. This wasn't what she was expecting, but it beat serving coffee. "Is it hard to learn?"

"Not at all. That's part of the beauty of our program." Honor's eyes glowed as he started talking about his creation. "It's very user friendly. It won't take you long to master it and learn the handbook and tools that teach it to the clients. Then I will start bringing you along to some meetings with school administrators and others we want to show it to. If you are as good at this marketing job as I feel you are going to be, I will eventually send you on your own to follow-up meetings to make sure things are going as planned."

"When you say go along, do you mean here in Carson's Bayou?" Callie tried to control the excitement in her voice. "Or will there be traveling?"

"It will be here in Carson's Bayou, of course, but we already have several schools across Louisiana, Mississippi, and Alabama looking at our software. Some are on board, but will still need a lot of excellent customer service over the next year while they learn the system. Others will need several visits to help them ensure they can use the software at its optimum level. Others will need help deciding whether our program is a good fit for their school. All of that will fall under the umbrella of your job."

"I can do this, Duck." Callie scooted to the edge of the chair and leaned toward the desk. Forget trying to be cool-headed. She wanted this job. "Give me a chance, and I'll show you. You know how good of a talker I am, and I can learn this stuff."

"So, I take it you are interested?"

"Yes." Callie nodded, leaning in toward the desk. "I can start tomorrow. I can even start today if you need me to." A smile spread across her face. "Oh, Duck, this is going to be great. You just wait. I'm going to wow you with my nerd-words and geek-speak."

"Let's start off by dropping the Duck. From now on, call me Honor." Honor rose from his chair. "Let me get you a new hire packet to fill out, then we will start on all the required orientation materials. That will get you to the end of today. Tomorrow morning, I will start teaching you the software."

Callie stood from her chair and waited as Honor came around the desk. "This is going to be great." She paused, catching herself before his nickname slipped from her lips. "Honor, thank you." She held out her hand. "I really want to give you a hug, like I used to when I passed a test after a tutoring session, but I know that's not professional."

"No, it's not." Honor shook her hand, then stepped back, and opened the door. "Clutch will get you started on the paperwork and give you a couple of polo shirts with our logo on the pocket to wear here in the office."

"Polo shirts." Callie's lips flattened into a thin line as Honor turned toward the door. Not exactly her style, but at least it wasn't a barista apron. "Can I wear jeans, or do I need to get khakis like yours?"

"I guess jeans will be fine as long as they aren't the ripped and holey kind."

Callie did a mental calculation of her wardrobe. She had one pair of jeans that would work. She would figure something out. She actually had a real job, even a job that could turn into a career. "Du—I mean, Honor." Honor turned. Callie bumped his shoulder and took a step backwards. "Sorry. Is marketing something you can study in college? You know, get a degree in?"

"Sure. Business and marketing degrees are great majors. Why?"

"No reason. I guess nobody applied for the job with that degree."

"No. They didn't."

Callie waited while Honor got the new employee pack from a file in the front office, then followed him into a room with a plastic table in one corner and a Coke machine in another. No need to tell Honor that she was planning on working a year, then quitting to go to school. This job would help her decide if marketing was something she wanted to get her degree in. If it was, next summer she would thank Duck for the work experience and turn in her resignation. In a couple of weeks, once she showed him how valuable she was going to be to his business, she would talk to him about the polo shirts and old lady jeans. Looking professional was one thing, looking frumpy was quite another.

onor looked at the clock on the corner of the computer screen. Callie had stepped in a few minutes ago to tell him she was leaving for the day. He wanted to give her a few minutes to get in her car and drive off before he left, too. No need to give her the impression that he was hanging around waiting for her to go first. He was, but no reason to give her that impression.

Geek-speak. He chuckled. Yeah, she was going to be great at this job. He switched off his computer screen and stood from his chair.

"I'm meeting a couple of people from the church at the pizza place," Clutch said, sticking his head through the office doorway. "You want to come along? It's Esther, the nurse practitioner, her brother, and a couple more."

"No." Honor flipped off his light and followed Clutch into the front office. "I'm going to go for a run, then head home. I have got to start unpacking the boxes stacked everywhere around my house. I'm spending too much money on paper plates and takeout food. I need to find my skillet so I can start making grilled cheese sandwiches again."

"I started to ask Callie if she wanted to join us, but I figured I'd better wait until she gets settled in a little better."

"You're not thinking of asking her out, are you?" Honor's eyebrows pulled down.

"Why?" Clutched grinned as they stepped onto the sidewalk and Honor locked the door behind them. "You said you weren't interested in her. She's just a friend."

"She is, but we are her bosses. I don't want you to scare her off."

"Yeah, we don't want that." Clutch chuckled. "Don't worry, man. I will stay away."

Honor ignored his friend's ribbing and said goodnight. He didn't have any feelings for Callie other than friendship, but Clutch didn't need to start anything with her, either. He would leave in a few months to go back to Houston, and Callie would be here. Clutch had that Clark Kent thing going on behind his big horn-rimmed glasses. He was way more Callie's type, but that wasn't the point. She worked for them. It wouldn't be right for either of them to be more than a boss, and, of course, a friend.

Honor pulled into his new house on the quiet street and hurried in to change. The little old lady across the street, Mrs. Albertson, had brought him over a container of homemade peanut butter cookies when he first moved in last month. Since then, she had also brought homemade mac and cheese and some brisket. He definitely had to keep the afternoon runs up with her around, or he would soon be putting the weight back on that he had carried with him when he lived in Carson's Bayou before.

When he and his dad moved to Houston after his mother moved out, his father had insisted that they both join a gym. He insisted it was an activity they could do together, and that Honor needed to do something besides schoolwork and play video games all day. His father had been right. Running had become a passion, and the overweight kid he had always been soon melted away. He stepped out of his front door and stretched before starting out for his five-mile run around the neighborhood. One thing about it, if you could run in the

Louisiana heat in the middle of the summer, you could pretty much run anywhere.

Mrs. Albertson waved as he ran by. "Don't you get over-heated, son," she called from her front steps. "I've got someone I want you to meet."

Honor waved, but kept running. A matchmaker. Oh well. He took her food without complaining. He would let her tell him about her lady friends too, but right now, a girlfriend was not on his radar.

CHAPTER SEVEN

*C*allie pulled the left-over container of ribs from her fridge, along with a container of potato salad, and another of watermelon. She stuck the ribs in the microwave and pulled a paper plate from her cabinet. She needed to go shopping, but not for food. Who cared about food? She could always bum a meal off Fiona. No, she needed clothes. Adult clothes. Clothes that a professional woman would wear to a business meeting. She dumped a glob of potato salad on her plate and waited for the microwave to ding. The great thing about potato salad was that it tasted just as good the second day as it did the first. She licked the back of her spoon as she put the lid on the container. It was a good thing too. Langston had noticed the mustard she added after all and hadn't eaten any, which meant more for her to bring home.

The microwave dinged, and she pulled out the ribs and slid them onto her paper plate. She grabbed a soda from the fridge and stepped the few feet over to her futon that served as her couch and her bed. She only had forty bucks in her checking account, but payday was coming. She plopped her plate down beside her and grabbed the piece of paper from the purse at her feet. The ribs needed to cool, and she needed to ogle her new salary. She had never made more than minimum wage in her life, and her bank account was always somewhere between drained and bleeding red. If she was careful, and she would be, that was another thing that was changing today. No more thoughtless spending. With adult wages came adult responsibilities. But if she was careful, she could build up a decent credit score and get a nice little used car before she left for LSU next year.

She picked up a rib from her plate and took a bite of the slow cooked meat that was falling off the bone. The tan polo shirt and sensible jeans hung on the bathroom doorknob across the studio apartment. A boring sign of her life to come... her life of increased wealth and influence ... and her ticket out of Carson's Bayou. The corners of her lips turned up in a smile. Barbecue sauce dribbled down her chin, and she made a mental note to pick up a Tide pen at the dollar store. Clutch had only given her two shirts, and she was sort of notorious for spilling stuff on her clothes. The last thing she needed was to stain up her work shirt and have to wear something else. Then again... no, better not risk it. She would follow the rules for workplace attire, at least until she made herself indispensable.

"Benny and the Jets" blared out from her cell phone, and she looked down at the unknown number. *Switch all my ringtones to professional ones before I start work*. She licked her finger and pushed the answer button.

"Callie."

"Dawson." Callie let out a long huff of air. What did he want now? Nothing she needed to bother herself with. "Look." She lifted her plate of food from her lap and set it on the futon beside her. "I said we could be friends, but the truth is, I really don't want to talk to you. I thought you would figure that out when I blocked your number."

"Aw, Callie. Don't be like that. I'm going to be moving to Austin soon. I got that football scholarship after all."

"That's good, Daw. I'm happy for you. I really am." Callie leaned over and picked up her sweaty Dr. Pepper bottle from the floor beside her foot. "I hope everything works out for you, but we've talked about this. You and I, we are on different paths now. It's better for both of us if we just move on, make a clean break."

"Cal, come on." Dawson's voice took on the hurt tone that always made Callie feel like a heel. "Nobody understands me like you do. You know that. I'm not asking you to take me back or anything. Can't we get together one more time so I can leave for UT knowing we are still friends?"

Callie laid her head back against the futon and stared at the ceiling. It probably wouldn't hurt to see him one more time. She was definitely over him, that was for sure, so no worries about falling into those old habits. If she went out with him this one last time and explained that she had no intention of getting back with him, maybe he would leave her alone. "Well." She lifted her head, and her eyes roamed the small apartment she had grown to love. She stopped at the ugly tan polo across the room. Did she really want to slide backwards when she was moving forward? "No, Dawson. I can't."

"Why not, Cal? You know you want to."

"No, Dawson, that's the thing. I really don't. Besides, I've started a new job and have a lot of stuff to learn. I don't have time to go out, even if I did want to, which I don't."

Callie rolled her eyes and flopped her head back against the futon as Dawson went on and on about how he needed to see her just one more time. She picked up a rib and took a bite, waiting for him to take a breath. "Are you about done? Because I need to go."

"You didn't use to be like this, Callie. You used to be fun."

Callie pulled the phone from her ear and pushed the red button, ending the call. "I also used to be stupid, you big oaf." She tossed the rib bone on her plate, her appetite suddenly gone. She got up and stepped across to the kitchen, tossing the plate of food in the trash can. She put the recycled butter bowl full of watermelon back in the refrigerator for later. Her phone buzzed again, and she stepped over and picked it up. "Hello."

"Callie." A deep, familiar voice filled her ear. "It's Honor."

A smile tugged at the corner of Callie's lips, and she tucked a stray piece of hair behind her ear. "You can't fire me, or unhire me, or whatever. I've already signed the paperwork."

"Don't worry about that. You are now an official Honor Systems employee. I was calling to make sure Clutch told you what time to be at the office in the morning?"

"Eight, right?"

"Yeah, that's right."

"I'll be there in my lovely tan shirt, eager to learn."

"Alright." Silence. "Well."

Callie waited, a slight tingle running across her neck at the sound of Honor's deep voice, so different from Dawson's whine from a few minutes before. "Duck." She eased down to the futon, tucking her feet underneath her. "Thank you for giving me a chance."

"You're welcome. See you tomorrow."

"This hasn't been nearly as boring as I thought it would be." Callie leaned back in the metal folding chair and stretched her arms above her head. "But you really need to think about getting me a better chair. This one is brutal on my behind."

"Let's take a break." Honor glanced at the clock in the corner of the computer screen. "We've been at it for three hours. Go grab an early lunch. When you get back, we will switch seats. You are catching on to this program fast."

Honor glanced over at Callie, pulling her shoulders back and stretching her arms behind her. He cleared his throat and opened his desk drawer, pulling his eyes away from the way her body filled out her polo shirt. "I got you a little present to help celebrate your first day on the job."

"Really?" Callie quit twisting like a contortionist and leaned over, brushing up against Honor's shoulder. "You didn't have to do that. What is it?"

"Close your eyes." Honor kept his hand inside the desk where Callie couldn't see what he held and waited for her to comply. His eyes twinkled with mischief as she sat up straight in the chair, eyes closed. She held out both of her hands, palms up, waiting for his gift. "Here you go. I also brought some milk, a bowl, and a spoon and left them in the kitchen."

Callie looked down at the little brown package of instant oatmeal in her hands and her laughter filled the office. "Cinnamon Swirl. And you even got the Good Value brand, too." She dropped her hands into her lap and looked up at Honor. "You might not believe me, but I haven't eaten this stuff in years."

"You're right. I don't believe you."

They both looked at the door as Clutch stepped through, holding an enormous bouquet of pink and white roses. "These were just delivered for a Miss Callie Madison," he said, setting the glass vase down on the corner of Honor's desk. "Looks like somebody is happy you got this job."

Callie's eyes stretched wide. She looked from the flowers

to Honor, her eyebrows raised in question. "From you?"

"I got you the oatmeal. Remember?"

Callie hurried around the desk and leaned over the flowers, breathing in their fragrance. "They must be from Fiona and Langston. I have the sweetest family." Her top teeth nibbled on her lower lip as she searched through the bouquet for the card.

Honor leaned back in his chair, his gaze fixed on Callie as she opened the tiny envelope and read the note. The joy on her face melted away as her eyes scanned the words. "You okay?"

"Huh?" Callie looked up from the card, and a stiff smile replaced the worried frown. "Oh. Yes. They are from an old friend." She slipped the card into her back pocket and looked at Clutch. "You want to put these in the lobby on that little table in front of the window? It looks kind of naked when you're walking by on the sidewalk."

"Uh, sure." Clutch shrugged his shoulders and glanced at Honor, who shrugged back. "If that's what you want."

"I think it would help make this place look a little more inviting from the outside until you can get a plant or something to put there."

"Good idea." Honor rolled his chair back from the desk and stood. "Remind me when you get back from lunch to call the florist and get some kind of fake plant to put in there."

"Fake?" Callie wrinkled her nose. "Get a real one. A fake one will be so... fake."

"Are you going to make sure it stays alive?" Honor stepped around his desk and looked down at the roses, rubbing a leaf between his fingers. "You don't have to water a fake plant."

"Geesh." Callie rolled her eyes and stepped toward the door. "Put it on my list of duties, boss. I can handle keeping the office plant alive."

Honor watched Callie step into the hall, her purse on her shoulder. He listened as she asked Clutch how long she had for lunch, then left, the front door whooshing behind her. Who had sent the flowers? An old boyfriend? A current boyfriend she was fighting with?

It didn't matter. He looked back at his desk to the pack of oatmeal laying near the computer, forgotten. He had grabbed it from his cabinet on a whim this morning when he was fixing his lunch. Obviously a dumb thing to do. He picked it up and stuck it back in his desk drawer and headed to the kitchen.

Yesterday after his evening run, he had come home to his empty house, and for the first time since his breakup with Sheila, loneliness had washed over him like a cold winter rain. He had called his dad but got his voicemail. Since he had remarried last year, he was harder and harder to keep up with. Honor didn't mind. His dad deserved happiness, and Dana made his father laugh more than his mother had ever done. He had thought about calling Clutch but remembered he was out with friends. That's when he called Callie. He had put her number in his phone before leaving the office, in case he ever needed to reach her. When she answered, he realized how dumb it was to call his new employee out of the blue.

He pulled his ham and cheese sandwich from the break room refrigerator and stepped to the front office. She was right. The flowers looked good in the window. He looked through the glass across the street to where Callie sat in her beat up old Beetle, her cell phone against her ear, a frown on her face. His eyebrows pulled down as he watched her raise her hand in frustration, arguing with whoever was on the phone. He turned and headed back to his office, unwrapping his sandwich. *Boundaries, Honor. This is not high school, and she will not appreciate you sticking your nose in her personal life. A pack of oatmeal. What was I thinking?*

CHAPTER EIGHT

"I was so nervous." Callie looked over to Honor behind the wheel of his old Subaru. A dark curl fell recklessly forward over his brow. "But this turned out to be fun." The dimples in her cheeks appeared as her lips stretched into a smile. "I've come a long way in a short time."

"You have." Honor glanced at Callie, then turned his eyes back to the road, pulling out of the parking lot of the Bridge-water High School onto the street. "I knew you would have a knack for the presentation part, but you have also done remarkably well learning the computer program over the last two weeks."

Callie straightened the seat belt draped across her cream-colored satin blouse and black fitted blazer. She didn't want the car's prickly old material to snag her new work clothes. "The power point presentation was no problem, but I have an idea about how we can make things better, if you want to hear it."

"Sure, but before you get into it, is the Olive Garden okay for dinner?"

"You buying?" Callie ran her hands over her black pants,

careful not to look in Honor's direction. She would love to eat at Olive Garden, but if the money was coming out of her pocket, Chic Filet would do just fine.

"Yes, I'm buying. Or I should say that it is a business expense."

"Then Olive Garden is great." Callie felt Honor's eyes boring into her. "What?" she asked, raising her chin and meeting his gaze.

"Nothing." The corners of Honor's lips twitched, but he turned to look at the road where the light had turned green. "What is this idea of yours?"

"I think you should bring a couple of laptops along already set up with the programs. Have a couple of fake students for the people to work on. One of a child who is doing very well in school, and another of a child with some sort of learning setback like dyslexia or ADHD or something. Let the staff actually sit down and look at the ways the program can be fitted for each individual child's needs and how easily it can be adapted for the teacher as well."

"That's not a bad idea," Honor said, surprise obvious in his voice. "We could have a couple of teachers or social workers looking at the mock lesson plans on our program after the presentation while we are answering questions and reviewing the software." He pulled into the parking lot of the restaurant and put the car into park. "As a matter of fact," he reached up and began loosening his tie. "That is such a good idea that I may even buy you dessert."

Callie watched as Honor threw his tie in the back seat where he had put his suit coat earlier. He stepped out into the black, starless night and walked around the car and opened her door. She had met him at the office at one that afternoon, and they had driven the three hours to Bridgewater. This had given them an hour to set up the room for the presentation. The presentation had also taken an hour, but by the time they stood around and talked to the principal and several of the school board members, and then packed everything back up, it was after seven when they got to the restaurant. They probably wouldn't get back to Carson's Bayou until after midnight, but it was Friday night, and she could sleep in tomorrow.

Callie was actually thankful to be out of town tonight anyway. After Dawson sent the roses a couple of weeks ago, he had called several times asking her out. She had put him off, but yesterday when she left for lunch, he had pulled in behind her at the Gumbo Hut.

"Come on, Cal." Dawson held the door open for Callie as she walked into the restaurant to pick up her order of fried pickles and sweet tea. "I'm leaving in a few weeks. Go out with me just one more time tomorrow night."

"I can't, Dawson. I'm busy." Callie stepped up to the register and gave the cashier her called in order. "And Saturday I'm babysitting, so don't even ask." She pulled her wallet from her purse and slid the money across the counter. She turned to where he was propped next to her. She noticed a new tattoo of bull horns, University of Texas's logo, on his muscular forearm. "Please stop calling me. I'm not in college anymore, and it is not cute for you to follow me around like this."

"Are you going out with that boss of yours?" Dawson leaned over and pulled a toothpick from the dispenser. "What kind of name is Clutch anyway? That can't be the guy's real name."

"No, I'm not going out with Clutch. Not that it's any of your business. I'm working." The woman behind the counter handed Callie a brown paper bag and an enormous Styrofoam cup. "Please, Dawson. Don't make this weird. Go to UT, do well, have a great life. Just don't call me anymore."

She had left him standing there, propped against the

counter with a toothpick hanging out of the corner of his mouth. At least he hadn't tried calling her again. Maybe he was finally getting the hint.

"Callie."

"Hmm?" Callie blinked and looked over at Honor as they slid into a booth. The smell of yeasty baked bread filled her nostrils. She looked around at the tables full of couples of all ages filling the restaurant. The lack of country music coming from a jute box or the distinct and although pleasant smell of fried pickles was a welcomed change from her usual date night destination of the Gumbo Hut. Of course, this certainly wasn't a date. "I'm sorry. I was thinking about how well everything went tonight. What did you say?"

"I asked you if working on a Friday night was interfering with your social life? Unfortunately, when setting up these meetings with the schools, we are at their mercy, and a lot of them meet on Fridays."

"Actually, no, this worked out great." Callie watched as Honor slid into the booth across from her. "I never get to leave Carson's Bayou, so I was looking forward to getting out of town." She looked down at the napkin sitting on the table, then back over to Honor. "That sounds kind of pitiful, doesn't it?"

"No, not pitiful, just honest." Honor waited while the waitress handed them a menu. He ordered water with lemon, and Callie ordered a Dr. Pepper. "Since we are being honest, I will tell you that I'm glad you are here with me. Making this trip by myself would have been pretty boring."

"It was fun talking about the old days." Callie looked down at the menu and frowned. "Uh, Honor." She laid the menu down and leaned forward. "I know you're going to think I'm a childish country hick, but I've never eaten at an Olive Garden before. I don't have a clue what half of this stuff is."

Honor's eyes softened, and he looked down at the menu. "Why don't you allow me to order for both of us? If I remember correctly, you don't care for shrimp, but love chicken and anything in tomato sauce, right?"

"How do you remember all of this stuff about me, Duck?" Callie's eyes sparkled. "I mean Honor."

"I was a shy kid, remember? Not a lot of friends?"

"Yeah, I guess." Callie's eyebrows pulled together. "Was it hard moving to another school where you didn't know anybody?"

"It was." Honor smiled up at the waitress and gave her their order. When she was gone, he picked up a breadstick the woman had set in the middle of the table. "My dad did everything he could to make it easy on me. I actually saw more of him then than when him and Mom were together. I think he stayed away from home to avoid the fighting."

"I had no idea you had all of that going on." Callie followed Honor's lead and took her own breadstick. Her stomach growled, and she pressed a hand down on her gut, trying to make it behave. "You never talked about it or acted down or anything at school."

"It wasn't that bad, really. Dad stayed away, and I thought it was normal that he was working and too busy to be around. When we moved to Houston, we started doing stuff together, like going to the gym and eating dinner together." Honor laid the rest of the breadstick on the plate and wiped his fingers on his napkin. "If we hadn't moved to Houston, I never would have gotten so involved in computers and ended up with the scholarship or building the business I have now. Plus, I met Clutch. He got me involved in church. That helped a lot."

"That reminds me." Callie took a sip of her Dr. Pepper from the sweaty glass. "Is Clutch his real name? I've never met anyone named Clutch before."

"Yep," Honor nodded. "He's the one and only. It's on his driver's license and social security card. We met my first day of school in Houston. The calculus teacher told him to show me around. I guess the old guy figured we would hit it off. I was a pudgy computer geek, and Clutch was a skinny math nerd. We've been best friends ever since."

"Wait." Callie's brow arched. "Clutch was a skinny nerd? I know you were a little roly-poly because I was there, but it's hard to believe Clutch was ever skinny." Callie's eyes roamed from Honor's dark wayward curls to his five o'clock shadow across his square chin and on down to his white dress shirt stretched over his broad shoulders and muscled arms. She jerked her eyes back up to meet the smirk on Honor's face. "Well. You know what I mean. You've changed a little since then, but I can't imagine Clutch not looking like, well..."

"Superman?" Honor raked his fingers through his dark waves and shook his head. "If I didn't know him better, I would think that's why he wears those black horn-rimmed glasses. But it's not. He's always worn those things, even when he was a skinny, pimple-faced junior in high school. He wanted me to go to church with him, but I was not interested. I was a new kid in a new town, and you know I'm not a social kind of guy. He kept at me until I finally agreed to go on the condition that he would start going to the gym with me and my dad. I figured it would get him off my back, but it didn't. He started meeting me and Dad at the gym in the afternoons, so I had to go to church with him. His dad wasn't in the picture, so I think he enjoyed getting to know my father."

The waitress appeared at their table and placed a fragrant dish of chicken parmigiana with creamy fettuccini noodles in white sauce on the side in front of Callie. "This looks heavenly." She tilted her head upward, her nostrils flaring as she breathed in the aroma of marinara, melting cheese, garlic and other spices all blending together to tempt her palette. "I skipped lunch because I was afraid I would spill something on my top and be a mess before the presentation." She picked up her fork and ran her tongue over her upper lip. "Let's eat."

Honor reached over and placed his fingers lightly on Callie's hand. "Do you mind if I say grace before we start? It will only take a second."

"Uh." Callie laid down her fork, very aware of the warmness of Honor's fingers against her skin. "Sure. No problem."

CHAPTER NINE

*H*onor pulled his hand back, bowed his head, and said a brief prayer of thanks for the food, the success of the night, and the friendship he shared with Callie. He lifted his head and looked into Callie's blue eyes, staring at him, wide and unreadable. "What? Did I do something wrong?"

"No." Callie's words stumbled, a grimace forming on her face. "I've never." She turned her eyes away and picked up her fork, slowly lifting her face back to Honor. "I imagine you are the first person ever to thank God for having me as a friend." Her shoulders lifted in a small shrug and she turned her face back to her food. "This looks so good," she said, her voice a little shaky. "I can't wait to taste it."

Honor stared at the top of Callie's head, bent over her plate, his shrimp scampi forgotten. "What makes you say that? You used to have a ton of friends. I've changed a lot since high school but you." He paused, taking in her blond curls falling over her narrow shoulders, held away from her face with simple gold barrettes. Her chin tilted up, and her china-blue eyes watched him as he took in the beauty of her face. "If anything, you look even more lovely now than you did back then." He cleared his throat and forced his lips into an amiable smile. "What's not to like? I can't imagine you not having a lot of friends."

"You really are my friend, aren't you?" Callie swallowed hard, not following his attempt into light-hearted banter. "Fiona is my friend, and her husband Langston is, too. Sidney is a combination of over-protective big brother slash father figure. I guess that's all the people in my life who are truly my friends."

"I understand what you are saying." Honor's eyes narrowed. "You have a lot of acquaintances, but only a few real friends."

"Yes. Sort of." Callie pulled in a deep breath of air and laid her fork back on her plate. "Honor, I guess you need to hear this from me because I'm sure you will run into people around Carson's Bayou who will love to fill your ears with a lot of stories."

Honor reached across the table and placed his hand over Callie's. "You don't have to tell me anything. Things happen from time to time. That's life, Cal. I know the real you, the soft and squishy you, remember?"

"The oatmeal me." Callie's face softened. "The truth is, I was not the nicest person in college. Some days I felt like I was going to war, and... well, let's just say that I attacked first instead of waiting for the enemy to have a chance to hurt me." She swallowed again and picked back up her fork. "Anyway I'd better eat this food before my stomach starts singing like a walrus in heat."

Honor squeezed Callie's hand, then pulled his arm back across the table. "We can't have that now, can we?"

"So." Callie paused and put a bite of the chicken in her mouth. A look of pure pleasure took over her face. She rolled her eyes back letting out a groan.

"You like it?" Honor asked, enjoying Callie's display of pleasure.

"You can order for me anytime." Callie rubbed her lips together and began cutting her chicken for a second bite. "So, you asked me about my social life. Now it's your turn. Are you putting off a hot date so you can get this meeting done tonight?"

Heat crept up Honor's neck, and he looked down at his food. "No, I'm still flying solo." He stuck his fork into a shrimp and held it up, examining it, keeping his eyes away from Callie's inquisitive stare. "I dated a girl, but we broke it off a while back. I decided to take a break from socializing."

"A while back?" Callie held up her fork with the piece of chicken dripping with marinara sauce and melting cheese. "Last month, last year, last week? How long is a while back?" She lifted the food to her lips. "Oh, shoot." Marinara sauce dripped from the tip of the fork onto her blouse like a red-orange teardrop. "Why can't I eat a meal without dropping something on my shirt?" She stuck the bite of food in her mouth and dropped her fork back on the plate. "Remind me when we get back in the car to rub that with my Tide pen. Geesh." She picked the napkin up from her lap and scrubbed the red spot on her chest. "This is the nicest blouse I own."

"Do we need to go?" Honor swallowed the food he had finally put in his mouth and dabbed his lips with his napkin. "We can get to-go boxes."

"No, unless your sloppy employee is embarrassing you."

"I seriously doubt you could ever embarrass me." Honor put his napkin back on his lap and retrieved his fork. "Besides, that little spot is barely noticeable."

"Are you kidding me?" Callie stared across the table, her lips poking out like a duck. "I need a bib. Oh well, as Nana used to say, 'it is what it is.' I will not let my dribbling like a baby ruin my evening."

"That's the spirit." Honor grinned as Callie finished the chicken and attacked the fettuccini with a vengeance. "This wouldn't be nearly as good reheated in the microwave."

Callie swallowed the cheesy noodles and took a sip of her Dr. Pepper. "Now. Back to the question. How long have you been flying solo?"

"Let's see." Honor sipped his ice water and pretended to ponder his answer. "A little over a year, I think." *A year, three months, and two weeks.* He had figured it up earlier that day when he was getting ready to meet Callie. He had actually changed shirts three times and slapped on some cologne before he realized what he was doing. *Tonight is strictly business, man. Chill out.*

"I'm not looking for a girl at this stage in my life," he said, watching his hand set his water glass, slippery with condensation, back on the table. "I have to get this branch of the business up and running." He looked back across the table, wishing the conversation would take a turn away from where it was headed. "After everything is stable, then I might devote more time to my personal life."

"Yes, heaven forbid you actually try to do both things at once."

"Speaking of business. Tell me more about setting up these demonstration computers. I would like to get started on that so we can try it out on our next clients."

"We are going to look like a couple of drowned rats." Callie stared out the door of the restaurant to the torrent of rain coming down in the inky night sky. "Oh well, might as well make a run for it."

"No." Honor put his hand on Callie's elbow as she pushed her shoulder against the glass door. "I'll get the car and come pick you up. Wait here."

"You don't have to do that." Callie looked up at Honor, his arm brushing against hers. "I won't melt in the rain. Besides, we are going back to Carson's Bayou after this. It won't matter what I look like on the ride home, even if it is a drowned rat."

"Yeah, but it's a three-hour ride. You might catch a cold riding all that way in wet clothes."

"The same thing applies to you."

"No need for both of us being sick. Wait here. I'll be right back."

Callie watched the hard-headed man dart out the door and disappear into the downpour before she could argue again. She reached over and touched her arm where his hand had been. He really was a dear friend. Who else would run through a storm to get the car for her? Certainly not Dawson Wallace.

A few minutes later, the Subaru pulled up in front of the entrance as planned. Callie pushed against the door but stared in amazement as Honor jumped out of the car and ran around to open the passenger's side door, soaking himself again. *Okay. Now you're just being ridiculous.* She hurried out and slid onto the car seat, watching as Honor, drenched to the bone, his white shirt sticking to him like a clingy piece of cellophane, slammed her door and hurried around to the driver's side.

"You didn't have to get out the second time." Callie dusted the few droplets of rain from her shoulders and looked over at the man sitting beside her, soaked completely through. Dark curls plastered his forehead, and rivers of rainwater ran down his face.

"I was already wet, so what was a little more rain?"

"Well, you are Duck, after all." Callie reached over and pushed a wet strand of hair away from his eyes. "A little water can't bother you."

Honor looked at Callie, and a mischievous grin crept onto his face.

"You wouldn't dare," Callie said, as a wicked smile turned up the corners of his mouth.

He began shaking his head and shoulders every bit as hard as a Golden Retriever after a swim in a pond. Water flew from his head like a fire hose, dousing Callie with a light shower.

"Duck! You're, you're..."

Honor stopped and laughed, a deep chuckle bursting from his chest. "What? Your knight in shining armor? Your hero? A humble saint sacrificing his comfort to help a lady in need?"

"Definitely not." Callie leaned over and punched him in the shoulder. "I don't know what you are, but I've been thinking." She tugged the ancient seatbelt across her chest and buckled herself in as he wiped a few puddles of water from his face and pulled the old car onto the street for the journey home. "We need to find you a girlfriend."

"We?" Honor raised an eyebrow and glanced at Callie. A drop of water trickled down to the tip of his nose. "I am quite capable of finding my own girlfriend when the time comes." His teeth started to chatter, and shivers became visible through his soppy wet shirt. "I don't need any help. But thanks for the offer."

"Oh, Duck." Callie laid her hand against his face, his slight shadow of whiskers feeling rough against her palm. "You're freezing. We have to get you warm, or you really will be sick." She reached over and turned on the heat with her other hand. A pitiful moan came from somewhere in the car's dash as tepid air began to blow.

"I'll be fine," he said, his face turning into her hand of its own accord.

His lips brushed against her palm, and a different sort of shiver ran down Callie's arm. She pulled back her hand. "Let's go through that Starbucks and get a coffee," she said, pink creeping into her cheeks. "That will heat you up."

Why was she blushing? This was Duck for goodness sakes. She reached down and grabbed her purse from the floorboard. She sat back and pretended to search through its messy contents for the Tide pen while watching him from the corner of her eye. He was definitely nice looking. Clutch had that in your face wake up gorgeous kind of good looks. Dawson had the bad boy handsome thing going on, but Honor. Callie chewed on her lower lip, watching as he rubbed his hand across his jaw. Standing next to the other two, you might not notice him at first, but after a second look…. She pulled in a deep breath as she watched a drop of water run down his cheek, across the curve of his jaw and onto his neck, disappearing into the collar of his shirt. *Get your head on straight, Callie. You are moving in a year, and besides, this is Duck. He's the last person you need to be daydreaming about.*

A few minutes later, Callie wrapped her fingers around the hot cup of coffee. "It's starting to get a little warmer in here, but really, Duck." She glanced around at the worn-out interior of the Subaru. The dash was faded with a couple of small cracks in the vinyl. The cloth on the roof was spattered with stains, and the leather seats were tearing open at the seams. "This car has about had it."

"Don't be talking smack about the Subaru." Honor took a sip of the coffee then held the cup up to his cheek. "She's been good to me. I'm not going to abandon the old girl just because she's got a few miles on her."

"Well, at least bring the thing by Sydney's shop and let

him fix the heater. It sounds terrible, like a dying moose or something." She watched him take a second sip of his coffee. "I really hope you don't get sick. Are you starting to warm up?"

"Yeah, I'm fine." He set his cup in the drink holder and glanced over at Callie. "It's not too hot in here for you, is it? That storm caused the temperature to drop, but it's not really that cold outside if you're dry."

"Quit worrying about me." Callie let out a yawn and laid her head back against the old leather seat. "My belly is full. I'm nice and dry. Hopefully, the coffee will kick in, or I might fall asleep on the ride home."

"Don't try to stay awake if you're tired." Honor followed the traffic onto the interstate, heading back to Carson's Bayou. "It's been a long day. Rest up. I'll get you home safely."

Callie smiled softly, watching Honor's shadow in the darkness. "I know you will, Duck."

CHAPTER TEN

*C*lutch scanned down the list of expenditures on his computer screen, then back up at Honor. "I have to say," he said, his eyes creasing with laughter. "I'm feeling a little hurt here lately. Like I've been getting the short end of the stick."

"Hmm?" Honor continued staring out the window, ignoring Clutch, and his attempt to get under his skin. That man was out there again, sitting across the street behind Callie's car. The flashy Mustang had showed up about thirty minutes before lunch a few days ago, parking behind the beat-up old Volkswagen Beetle. It had been there again every day since. "If you keep doing such a good job like you've been doing," he had said to Callie as she headed out the door to lunch that first day he noticed the car, "you can get you a shiny toy like that one parked behind yours in three or four years."

Callie had looked out the window, but her smile had dropped away, and a scowl had taken its place. "That car is nothing but trouble."

"Earth to Honor."

"Hmm?" Honor said again, pulling his eyes from the window and looking down at his friend. "What did you say?"

"I said, how come when *we* have to go out of town to do a presentation or whatever, all I get for dinner is a Big Mac and a Coke. I see from your expense receipts that you've upped your game over the past couple of months. PF Chang's, Olive Garden, Cheesecake Factory, a couple of steak houses, and a few other places I've never heard of." He leaned back in his chair and put his hands behind his head. "I'm hurt man. What's Callie got that I don't have? I could eat a steak every once in a while too."

"Shut-up, Clutch." Honor frowned down at his best friend. "She will hear you. These walls are thin." He glanced over to where Callie had disappeared a few minutes earlier into the little break area in the back. "She's doing a good job, and I want her to know it. She hasn't had a chance to eat at any of those places before, and I want her to enjoy herself. These past couple of months have been a whole new way of life for her."

"Like I said, man." Clutch sat up and put both hands over his heart. "You are wounding me deep."

Honor picked up a pencil from a cup on the desk and threw it at Clutch's head. "The next time we have an out-of-town meeting, we will get steak." He shook his head and looked back out the front window. "It's like working with a kindergartener sometimes."

Clutch leaned over and picked the pencil up off the floor where it had landed after the eraser bounced off his head. "Actually, I'm glad you are raising the bar a little. It's about time you started paying attention to the opposite sex. Stopped living like a hermit."

"You ready?" Callie stepped out of the break room and smiled at both men. "Clutch, you are going to love the Gumbo Hut. Their po' boys are better than that fancy place

Honor and I ate at in New Orleans over the weekend." She shifted her purse on her shoulder and stepped up next to Honor. "I'm going to have to join a gym or something if I want to keep fitting in my clothes. Since I started working here and eating out at all these fancy places every weekend, I've put on five pounds. It's a good thing the weather has turned cool." She tugged on the cream-colored sweater she was wearing instead of the required company polo. "Winter clothes are a lot more forgiving than summer clothes."

Clutch grinned as he stood from behind the desk. "I don't know, but I imagine eating at McDonalds would do the same thing if you were eating there every time." He looked at Honor, whose lips were pressed in a flat line. "If you have to eat out, might as well eat somewhere nice. Right, Honor?"

"Right." Honor glowered at Clutch. "We could just bring your lunch back to you, you know. You don't have to go with us, or you could skip lunch all together and get those changes made on the Preston account."

"Are you kidding?" Clutch stepped around the desk and opened the front door, letting in a rush of chilly autumn air. "Callie has been trying to get me over to this place for lunch for weeks. You can stay and work on that account, but a shrimp po' boy and a piece of apple pie are calling my name."

Callie stepped onto the sidewalk and looked across the street. She looked back at Honor and then Clutch as he locked the office door. "Uh. Do you mind if we go in one of your vehicles?" She glanced over her shoulder and then back at the two handsome men beside her. "Either one of you will literally have to fold yourself in half to fit into my backseat."

"Let's go in my truck," Clutch said, pulling his keys from his jeans pocket. "The Subaru isn't much bigger than your Beetle."

Honor watched Callie glance over her shoulder again and then smile. She took both men by the arm as they started up the sidewalk away from her car— away from the flashy Mustang parked behind her. They all three stopped and turned as the sound of squealing tires and the smell of burning rubber filled the air.

"He sure is in a hurry to leave," Clutch said as they watched the Mustang peel out in the opposite direction.

Honor stared at Callie's face as the car disappeared down the street. "Do you know that guy?"

"Yeah, and he's an idiot."

Callie's eyes lit up as she watched Clutch bite into the apple pie. "See. I told you this place was great. It's not much to look at, but the folks in the kitchen know their business."

"You're right." Clutch nodded and took another bite of the pie. "This place *is* great. Do they deliver?"

"I don't know, but they take call-ins. Let me ask the waitress." Callie stretched her neck and looked around the crowded restaurant, bustling with the usual lunch crowd. This was just the opening she was looking for.

Elda, their waitress, was a year older than Callie. They had met during her first year of college, before she had gotten involved with Dawson. Elda had been in Callie's child psychology class with a syllabus focusing on elementary education. Callie had taken the class because the teacher was supposed to be easy, and she was required to have a psych class. They had talked a few times, and Elda, although a little shy and mousy, seemed like a nice person. She was in the Baptist Student Union and had urged Callie to join their Wednesday night Bible study group. Callie had agreed to go, but had never gotten around to it. After that semester, their paths had not crossed again until last month when Callie found Elda working here.

Callie waved her arm and called Elda over to their table. She would make a perfect date for Honor. Callie had stopped in the Gumbo Hut for a glass of tea after work or to pick up a takeout order and made a point to talk to Elda each time. The woman wasn't dating anyone, being too busy with work and online classes since graduating from junior college. She was taking as many courses as the online curriculum from Southeastern University allowed and planned to take the rest at a satellite branch of the school an hour away. She seemed to be a nice, quiet homebody who loved Carson's Bayou, perfect for Honor.

Elda wasn't much in the looks department, but from what Callie had learned from Honor since he had come back to town, he didn't really seem to pay attention to how a woman looked, anyway. A few women were obviously flirting with Honor on different occasions when they were together on a work trip, and the women's attempts had gone completely unnoticed, or Honor was very good at ignoring them. Callie wasn't exactly sure which.

No, he was more about a person's character. If she could get the two of them together and let them see how much they had in common, then Honor would notice Elda. That's why she had arranged to have him and Clutch come eat lunch with her. If she just set Honor and Elda up on a blind date, Honor would skin her alive. But if she arranged a double date with her and Clutch and him and Elda, he would have to go. He was too nice of a guy to remain alone for the rest of his life, and there were too many ruthless women out there who would love to get their hooks into her sweet best friend. He had given her a great job and was treating her so well. She could at least do this for him.

"Elda." Callie smiled at the woman as she hurried over, a

pitcher of sweet iced tea in her hand. "I want you to meet two of my friends from work. This is Clutch Franklin and Honor Jacobs. They own Honor Systems Technology. It's a software company that helps with school lesson plans and curriculums." Callie stretched her eyes wide, and looked from Elda to Honor, like the thought had just popped into her head. "Elda is studying to be an elementary teacher. I bet she would love hearing about your company." She picked up her tea glass and stuck the straw in her mouth, staring innocently at Honor.

"Uh." Honor wiped his hands on a paper napkin and reached out to shake the waitress' hand. "Hello. Nice to meet you. How do you know Callie?"

"We took a class together, child psych," Elda said, setting down the tea pitcher to shake his hand. Elda smiled politely and waited for Honor to say something else.

Callie waited for Honor to say something else as well, but he smiled back at Elda, then picked up his spoon dipping it into his empty bowl of gumbo, raking the sides for the last scrap of food. *Oh, good grief. No wonder you don't have a girlfriend.* "Clutch." Callie set her glass down and turned to the gorgeous man sitting in the chair to her right. "I have a great idea. Since we are not going to be out of town this weekend with work, why don't the four of us get together and do something fun, like go to the movies or play goofy golf or something?"

Clutch coughed and sputtered and almost blew tea out of his nose. Callie quickly patted him on the back. She looked from Clutch, now grinning like a possum eating grapes, to Honor, who looked like a deer caught in the headlights, to Elda, who continued to smile politely, like this was all business as usual. "You okay? A piece of ice must have gone down wrong," Callie said, slapping Clutch on the back one more time with a little extra force.

"I have an even better idea." Clutch wiped his mouth with his napkin and looked up at Elda and then over at Callie. "Our church is having an open mike night this Friday, as Elda already knows."

"Oh." Callie's eyes stretched wide in genuine surprise this time. "You two already know each other?"

"Yes," Elda said, smiling at Callie. "We are in the same Sunday School class, and we both sing in the choir."

"That's nice." Callie looked over at Honor who was staring at her with his eyebrows raised, no longer even attempting to smile. "See, Honor, we all already know each other, so this will be loads of fun."

"As I was saying." Clutch looked at Honor with a devilish grin on his face, totally inappropriate for discussing a night out at a church function. "We are having an open mike night where our class and a few more people all bring food. We play music and talk and eat. It's really laid back, but a good time. It would be a great place for a first date." His grin stretched even wider as Honor's eyes stretched wider.

"I'm in." Callie winced as she felt Honor's shoe kick her in the shin. She pushed her lips into a tight smile, ignoring Honor's under the table protest, and looked up at the waitress. "How about you, Elda? It sounds like fun."

"I will be going anyway, so I guess so."

"Good," Clutch said, slapping his hands together and winking at Callie. "Honor and I will pick you ladies up Friday night at five. This is going to be a great double date."

CHAPTER ELEVEN

*C*allie looked around the elegant dining room with the twelve-foot ceilings and hardwood floors. When Clutch said they were going to a Sunday school thing, she assumed they would be going to a fellowship hall at his church. They actually ended up in a beautiful, two-story home on the nicer side of town.

She and Honor weaved their way between the chairs and groups of people scattered around the formal dining room to the table overflowing with finger foods. Someone had moved the table against the wall in front of a tall, slender window with silk drapes overlooking a manicured yard with a white picket fence. The gathering felt laid back and welcoming in spite of the expensive furnishings throughout the pre-civil war era home.

The smell of fresh baked brownies and apple fritters mingled with the aroma of barbecue sauce on chicken wings and homemade salsa, all causing Callie's stomach to growl. She picked up a Styrofoam plate and looked over the table. So many choices. Laughter and the strumming of guitars coming from the other side of the room near the empty fireplace pulled her attention. She turned toward the familiar voices. Clutch and Elda stood talking with Lucas Wade and several other people she didn't know, obviously enjoying themselves.

"So," Honor said, drawing her attention back to the buffet style spread of food. "My next-door neighbor is your brother-in-law's little brother? You have got to love small town life." He speared a sausage ball with his fork and put it on his plate. "I should have figured that out. Lucas said he remodeled this house himself when Mrs. Albertson brought me over to meet him. His last name is Wade. He has to be a part of Wade Construction."

"Who's Mrs. Albertson?" Callie dipped Fritos onto her plate and began covering them with cheese dip. "Is she here?"

"No. She's the old lady that lives right across the street from me." Honor added a chicken wing to his plate. "She's always bringing food over to my house. She also invited me to this church. When I went the first time with Clutch, she tried to get both of us to go home with her for dinner. She kind of reminds me of your nana."

Callie stepped further down the table and puckered her lips. "I will get the banana pudding if you get a piece of that chocolate pie. Then we can share with each other."

"That's fine by me." He leaned forward to get the slice of pie Callie wanted, but stopped as a woman's crystal-clear voice penetrated through the hum of talking, causing everyone to stop and listen. The corners of his lips turned up in a smile as Elda sang "In Christ Alone", accompanied by a couple of guitars, a mandolin, and even a ukulele. "It appears my date has a hidden talent," he whispered in Callie's ear, slipping the pie onto his plate. "Did you know she could sing like that?"

"No." Callie looked across the room. Tonight, Elda didn't look anything like the mousy woman in the apron that waited on them at the Gumbo Hut. Her hair hung in loose waves around her shoulders, and she practically glowed as her voice rang out through the room. Callie looked back at Honor as he watched Elda sing. A twinge of something unpleasant caught in her gut as admiration flashed in his eyes. "Um." She cleared her throat and pulled her gaze away from him. "I'm going to find a place to sit, but don't feel like you have to babysit me. You can go up front with Elda and Clutch."

"What?" Honor turned back from staring at Elda, his eyes questioning. "No." He studied Callie's face for a second, then his eyes searched the room. "I'm fine back here. There are a couple of chairs near the other wall. Let's go sit over there out of the flow of traffic."

"Don't you think you need to go sit up there by your date?"

"Na." The room broke out into applause as the song ended. "She seems to be doing just fine without me. Besides." He nodded his head toward the mike where Clutch was stepping up to sing a duet with Elda. "Your date is up there, too. Shouldn't you be up there crooning with Clutch instead of scarfing down cheese dip and banana pudding with me?"

"Probably." Callie grinned as they started toward the empty chairs. "But that banana pudding is calling my name, and I can't carry a tune in a bucket. Believe me. The last place I need to be is in front of a microphone."

"Cal?"

The muscles in Callie's shoulders tightened as the voice behind her said her name. It couldn't be him. She stopped and looked around. She had to be mistaken. He did not hang out with these people. He had never once attended church with her while they were dating. She wasn't wrong. "Hello, Dawson. Are you friends with Lucas and Vivian?"

"No." Dawson's eyes darted around the room, and he ran

his hand through the top of his sandy blond hair. "No, I just heard that you might be here." He shoved his hand down in the front pocket of his jeans. "I thought I would stop in. I've been hoping we could have a chance to talk."

"Hello. I'm Honor Jacobs. I don't believe we've met."

Callie's jaw tightened as she watched Honor hold his hand out to Dawson. Honor's words were friendly enough, but his tone was firm, not threatening, but not open either. Protective. That's how Honor sounded. Like he used to when she was in eighth grade and some of the tenth-grade jocks would try to hit on her. She would get so aggravated with him back then when he nosed into her business, but now….

Dawson shook Honor's hand, then turned his eyes back to Callie, not bothering to introduce himself. "Can we step out and talk for just a minute?" He looked around at the people listening as Clutch sang "It Is Well With My Soul". "Some place private?"

"We are getting ready to eat," Honor said, inserting himself into the conversation again. He tilted his head toward his plate of food. "Why don't you come by the office on Monday while Callie's at work? You can talk to her then."

"Callie." Dawson's brow drew down as his voice got slightly louder. "You don't want all these people knowing our business, do you?"

Is he threatening me? Callie's eyes narrowed. She set her plate in the nearby chair. "I'll be right back, Honor. Believe me. This won't take long." She glared at Dawson, her lips set in a straight line. "Come on. Let's get this over with."

74

Fifteen minutes. Callie said she wouldn't be long. A couple of men Honor had met briefly at a church service were now singing an upbeat David Crowder song. Someone had started playing a set of bongos. The rhythm of the drums, along with the thud of the base, seemed to count off the seconds of Callie's absence. He looked down at the uneaten chicken wing and other food on his plate, no longer holding any appeal.

Fifteen minutes was long enough. That man, whoever he was, had practically been stalking Callie for the past few weeks. He could tell from the way she acted when she saw the guy's Mustang parked in front of their office that she had no desire to talk to this man. Tonight, she hadn't wanted to go with him either. He weaved through the clusters of people, tossing the uneaten food into a trash can as he made his way to the foyer and out the front door. Somebody needed to set this guy straight on how to treat a lady.

Honor stepped onto the front porch that ran the length of the house. Fall was definitely in the air. He rubbed his hands up and down the arms of his gray long-sleeved thermal, pushing away the chill. With the time change, it was already dark outside, and the streetlights cast a faint yellow glow over the quiet neighborhood. Lucas Wade's house sat on the corner lot, and the party-goers' vehicles lined the street on both sides of his house.

Something warm brushed against Honor's pants. He looked down at the skinny old tabby cat weaving its way around his leg. "Which way did they go, Truman?" He mumbled, looking back up from the neighborhood stray to the cars and trucks up and down the street. A tense voice cut through the quiet night air, clashing with the music and friendly voices floating from the house. He searched down the street toward his house. He couldn't make out the color in the muted light, but a dark Mustang was parallel parked between an SUV and a double cab truck on the opposite side of the street.

He hurried off the porch and out the front gate as another voice rushed in his direction. That was definitely Callie's voice, not as loud as the other one, but she was mad about something.

"That's not the way it was, Dawson. You know it's not."

"All I know is that you said you were, then you weren't. Do your church friends know about it, Cal? That's what I want to know. Do they know?"

Honor stepped around the SUV to where Callie and this man, Dawson, were standing. Dawson leaned against his Mustang, his arms crossed over his chest. Callie's back, ramrod straight, pushed against the SUV. Whatever was going on here, Callie was not happy about. The man seemed to be baiting Callie, trying to make her react. He had been nervous when they were in the house around all the people, but out here in the shadows, he was in complete control.

"Callie?" Honor stepped out of the dim light. "You okay? You've been gone about twenty minutes."

"I'm fine, Duck." Callie's lips stayed in a thin line as she continued to stare at Dawson. "You're leaving now, aren't you, Dawson? One of the men at the party is a state trooper." She pushed up on her toes and looked up the street. "Yep. There's his patrol car over there. If he comes out here and finds the open beer in your car, I bet he'll make you do a breath test." She shrugged her shoulders and crossed her arms over her chest. "I am pretty sure I know what that test would say."

"How do you know there's open beer in my car?" Dawson glanced over his shoulder, searching for the trooper's car.

"There's always open beer in your car, Dawson." Callie stared at the hulking man, no fear in her voice, just anger. "I know you, remember?"

Honor stepped closer to Callie as Dawson pushed off his car and stood up straight. "I think she's right. It's time for you to go."

"I'll go." Dawson started around the front of his car to the driver's side. "But you think about what I said, Callie. I don't want to fight with you, but we are going to talk. You can count on it."

"I have said everything I need to say to you."

Honor put his arm around Callie's shoulders as they watched the Mustang back out into the street and peel off down the road, running the stop sign on the corner at the Wade house. "That jerk is going to get himself killed one day."

Callie leaned her head over on Honor's shoulder, melting against his side. "Do you mind if we don't go back to the party? I'm kind of done in."

Honor felt Callie's body tremble, and he squeezed her shoulder. "I live right down here," he said, nodding in the opposite direction from where Dawson had disappeared. "Why don't we grab a cup of coffee at my house, then I can take you home."

"That sounds perfect." Callie pulled in a deep breath of air as they started through the dark night toward the dim glow of the next streetlight in front of his house. "I need to explain to you about what you heard, Duck. It's not what you think."

"You don't have to explain anything to me, Callie. It's me, remember?"

CHAPTER TWELVE

*C*allie looked around the front porch of the one-story wooden house. A brown leaf skittered across the wooden planks of the floorboards with a puff of wind. The house wasn't nearly as large or as nice as the Wade house up the street. The cracked paint on the walls and shutters looked like they could use a coat of paint. The black shutters on the white house sitting in the plain yard with no shrubs or landscaping seemed sad, sort of forgotten.

Honor unlocked the front door in the glow of the porch light he had left on for his return, and Callie followed him into the living room. "Make yourself at home, and I'll get the coffee," he said, flipping the light switch on the wall beside them.

Callie's eyes roamed around as he walked across the room, the floor creaking as he stepped on a board near the sofa. He disappeared into the dim light of the next room. The entire house had a "Leave It To Beaver" vibe, but in a bare bones, not feeling all the love, sort of way. The white walls didn't contain a single picture or familiar item, and the highly glazed pine wood floors didn't have a rug to give the place a cozy, welcoming feel.

She stepped over to the blue sofa with a tiny floral design, causing the same floorboard to creak as it had a few seconds before with Honor. She ran her fingers along the rough material of its well-worn arm. The matching love seat sat at a right angle to the sofa and reminded her of the furniture she had grown up with. It was not the same color and in better shape, but it looked frayed and used. Definitely a blast from the past. The simple square light fixture overhead gave off a soft-white glow, and Callie imagined what the room could be with a little TLC. Nothing as grand as what they had left up the street, but the place could have charm if treated right.

"I don't have that creamer for the coffee that you guzzle every morning at the office," Honor said, poking his head through the large arched doorway leading into the adjoining dining area. "Do you want milk and sugar?"

"Hmm." Callie pressed her lips together and sat down on the corner of the sofa. "Do you happen to have a Dr. Pepper?"

"No, but I have a Coke."

"Perfect. I'll take that instead." Callie leaned back on the sofa and looked around the room again. "Something's missing in here," she called to Honor's disappearing back. *Actually, a lot's missing in here, but I won't go there.* Her eyebrows pulled low as she scanned the room, trying to figure out what was wrong. "You don't have a TV." She twisted around and looked at the wall behind her to make sure she hadn't missed it, even though the wall behind the sofa would have been an odd place to put a television. "Let me change that." She turned around and looked back toward the dining room. "You don't have a TV in here."

Honor stepped through the dining room into the living room. "You're right. No TV. I have a computer in one of the bedrooms and my laptop. I'm not a big TV person and can stream anything I want to watch on one of those, or even my phone." Honor sat on the loveseat adjacent to Callie. He placed her Coke on the glass-topped end table with the scarred wooden legs. Other than the sofa and love seat, the single end table and matching coffee table were the only furniture in the room. He looked over his shoulder at the built-in bookcases on both sides of the dining room doorway. "I have a lot of books to put back there, but they're still in boxes in one of the bedrooms."

"How long have you been here?" Callie followed his gaze to the empty bookshelves, then around to the window covered by a sheer white panel. The walls were white, the curtains were white, not a drop of color in the place except for the furniture. No wonder it looked so stark.

"The beginning of May. I drove down from Houston after the new year and purchased this place at the same time I bought the office." His eyes roamed around the bare walls. "I still have a lot of stuff to do, but I've been busy getting the office going and making sure the business was running smoothly." He leaned back on the loveseat and took a sip of his coffee. "Until last week, there were still boxes scattered all over the place in here."

"This would drive me nuts." Callie picked up her glass and wiped the dampness off the bottom. She looked at the ring on the glass tabletop. Coasters, but that was way down the list of what this room needed. "You need to get your house in order. Put a few pictures on the wall, a rug on the floor, a throw pillow on the couch. Make this place look like home."

"I guess so." Honor leaned over and sat his coffee mug on the end table. "I get up and go for a run every morning before I come to work, and, as you know, I'm gone most Fridays. I've started going to church on Sundays, so Saturdays are the only time I'm really here. I get on the computer and work then, or Clutch has me out doing something with him. I guess my house is just not on my radar."

"Was your place in Houston like this?" She paused and sipped her Coke, cutting her eyes up at Honor. "Bland?"

"No. Sheila, my girlfriend, helped me fix it up. You have to remember, it was me and Dad on our own for a long time. Dad didn't bring anything from our old house with Mom when we left Carson's Bayou. I think he was washing his hands of her and that life. He rented a tiny little unfurnished house. We started over with basically our clothes and the car." A nostalgic smile turned up the corners of his lips. "We actually sat on lawn chairs and slept on air mattresses for a couple of months while Dad was learning how to live without Mom. He said we were indoor camping." He paused and looked around the empty space. "This is a big step up from that."

"You really went through a lot back then." Callie stared across the short distance at the quiet man, seeing the teen boy that had disappeared from her life a few years ago—a lifetime ago. A tender smile softened her face. "I'm impressed. You have done so much on your own, but now you have me to help you. Why don't we have a house fixer-upper party? Just me and you. I can come over and get this place looking lived in, and you can." She paused, trying to think of some sort of compensation for her offer of help. "You can take me mattress shopping. I've been sleeping on a futon ever since I moved into Sid's apartment. I'm ready for an actual bed. My sister-in-law redid a metal bed frame she found in the attic at Nana's, our old house. They gave it to me, but I couldn't affor—I haven't taken the time to buy a mattress. I can help you with your house stuff, and you can help me buy a mattress."

"Are you sure you don't have something better to do with your Saturday?"

"Just laundry. I take it over to Fiona's to wash, but I can drop it off, and Fi will throw it in the dryer for me." *And fold it.*

"Okay, then." Honor reached over and grabbed his coffee, taking a large sip. "We can get started in the morning." He grinned as Callie's stomach let out a loud rumble. "Are you sure you don't want a grilled cheese sandwich? I could sure use one. I can fix us one while you text Clutch and tell him where we disappeared to."

"Well, if you are fixing you one, I could eat one. I guess I need to tell Clutch to take Elda home when they are done, too." Callie stood and picked her glass up from the coffee table. She wiped her palm across the wet ring left in its place. "I want to see the rest of your house."

"It's coming along." Callie set a small framed photo on the end table of boy Honor and his dad in fishing caps holding their poles in front of a crystal blue lake. She looked back at the bookcases, now holding books and model airplanes Honor had built as a kid. She had arrived at eight that morning after leaving her dirty laundry with Fiona, asking her to wash it for her while she went and helped Honor with a few things. They had dug through boxes and boxes of books and eventually found a few photos and other things from his past to give his house a homey look.

There was a picture of Honor and a woman with long brown hair and large glasses at a park, and another of them all dressed up at some kind of formal affair. The woman was attractive, but in a hidden sort of way. "This Sheila?" she asked, looking at the smiling faces in the photo. That uncomfortable feeling in her gut twisted again. "She's cute. Why did you break up with her?"

Honor stepped over from where he was sorting through his books by CS Lewis. "<u>The Silver Chair</u> is not with the rest of the books," he said, a frown on his face. "I can't put the series on the shelf without book four." He looked over Callie's shoulder, and she breathed in the fresh smell of his soap. "I wonder how it got put in a different box?" He leaned in and took the photo from Callie. "That was at a birthday party of a friend of hers." He tossed the photo back in the box at Callie's feet. "You haven't seen it, have you?"

"Seen what?" Callie turned, bumping into his chest to avoid tripping over the boxes they had dragged to the living room. A ripple of warmth moved across her where she brushed against him. She jerked back, stumbling over the box behind her.

Honor grabbed her shoulder to stop her fall. "Whoa," he said, helping her find her balance. "Don't trip and break an ankle."

The warmth of his hand through her t-shirt caused another sensation to form in Callie's stomach. A deep ache. A longing for more. "Seen what?" she asked again, the words squeaking out. She cleared her throat. "Oh, the book? No, but we will come across it." She stepped back slowly, putting a little distance between herself and her friend. Her boss. "So, why did you break up with her?"

"I didn't." Honor's eyes darted away from Callie's face and to the open boxes sitting around the floor. "She broke up with me and started dating that guy."

"The guy who had the birthday?" Callie's eyes stretched wide, and she looked back down at the photo lying in the box. "You are kidding. Were you two close friends?"

"The birthday guy? Na. I didn't know him that well." Honor stepped toward the window and bent down, lifting the lid of another box. "He was somebody Sheila had met online a few months before." He stood back up and yawned, stretching his arms, his muscles visible through the taunt material of the gray t-shirt. "Oh look." He leaned back down and pulled a book from another box at his feet. "Here it is."

Callie pushed all the questions popping into her head from her mind. Obviously Honor was not pining over his old flame. If he was, he sure had her fooled. That feeling, whatever it was when he grabbed her to stop her fall, well, she needed to ignore that completely. Geesh. "Hey, can I ask you something?" She looked at the bookshelves, now holding novels tediously arranged by author and series.

Honor turned from where he was now arranging his nonfiction section, which held everything from how to build model planes, to the manual for his Subaru, to a collection of books on theology. His accumulation of books on computers and other nerd stuff was another section entirely. "Yes." The word rolled slowly from his lips as the corner of his mouth tilted up in a smile. "You ask me stuff all the time, but when you ask me if you can ask me something, I get a little worried."

"I was just wondering." Callie's fingers fiddled absently with the knot tied in the tail of her tie-dyed tank top. "Are you doing okay? Financially, I mean." Her eyes darted around the room, avoiding his intense gaze. "I mean, is your business doing alright? You are stable and all?"

"Yes." Honor's entire face broke into a grin, and he wiped his hands on the dish towel he had been using to dust the books as he placed them on the shelf. "Why? Are you worried about your job security?" he said with a chuckle. He stepped over to the love seat where Callie was standing on the other side. "I assure you, your check will be deposited into your account every week like clockwork."

"No." Callie's lips puckered into a frown as she shook her

head. "You know I'm not worried about that. It's just." She reached down into the box on the couch and pulled out several eight by ten black and white photos of scenes around Carson's Bayou she had found earlier. They were shots taken around the town, but from years ago, maybe in the late eighties or early nineties. "We need to put something on that wall, and I don't think you want tons of pictures of you and your dad staring down at you every day."

"No." Honor looked at the wall where Callie was indicating. "That would be kind of weird. What does that have to do with my financial stability, or lack of?"

"I think we need to go to Hobby Lobby after we go look for my mattress." She held up a couple of the photos. "We could put all of these in matching frames and maybe get a shelf or two to put them on. It would give this room a lot more, um." She bit her lower lip and glanced over at his laughing face. "Character?"

"I can afford a few picture frames and anything else you think the house needs." He leaned across the love seat and looked at the photos. "My dad took these pictures when he first moved to Carson's Bayou. That's a great idea." He stood back up straight and raised an eyebrow. "Is there anything else you think I need?"

"Yes." Callie grinned. "Since you asked, you need some new curtains with a little color in them, those throw pillows I mentioned last night, a rug for the floor, a couple of candles, coasters, dish towels..."

"Why don't you make a list?" Honor smiled. "I'll call Clutch and see if I can use his truck for this trip. It sounds like everything might not fit in the Subaru."

CHAPTER THIRTEEN

"*Y*ou know what's more fun than shopping?" Callie piled the bags holding the new throw pillows into the back of Clutch's double cab truck on top of the one holding the new slipcovers for the couch and love seat.

"What?" Honor slid into the driver's seat and waited for Callie to get in. "A root canal?"

"No." Callie rolled her eyes and climbed into the truck. "Shopping with other people's money."

"I take it you don't spend your hard-earned dollars quite as easily as you are spending mine?" Honor pulled his seatbelt across his chest and buckled it in place. They had finished up working at his house around one and headed to Shreveport to get the things Callie wanted for his house. He had never been a shopper, never put a lot of thought into what was on his walls or how things looked. He was starting to see; however, that his environment needed more attention. Even in the office, since Callie had made the few changes like putting the plant in the window, the welcome mat out front, and hung the wooden sign with the company name on the wall as you walked into the building, the place looked like someone cared. Before, it looked more like an amateur workshop. Now it looked like professionals owned the place. He could tell from the people who came in that the place made them feel more confident in the people working there.

He hadn't given much thought to how his home looked, even less than the office, but since she had made the changes this morning, he could see how much the homey touches would affect him. Already, just having his books and other stuff out where he could see them made the house feel like a place where he wanted to be, where he lived. That's what he had been looking for when he came back to Carson's Bayou in the first place, a home, a place where he could connect with people and really put down his roots.

"Earth to Honor." Callie leaned over and waved her hand in front of Honor's face. "You in there somewhere?"

"Sorry." Honor grinned and started the truck engine. "I was thinking about how much work we accomplished this morning on the house. We got more done before lunch today than I have gotten done since May."

"Well, this is getting work done, too." Callie dropped her purse on the floorboard at her feet. "It's fun work, but it still has to be done. Let's see." She held up her hands and started counting off her list on her fingers. "We've gotten the frames and shelves and curtains and coasters and throw pillows and other stuff for the living room. We've gotten the dish towels and mug rack for the kitchen. We've gotten the thingy to hold your toilet paper for the bathroom and the stuff for the counter to put your toothbrush in and the hand soap dispenser and the matching hand towels." Her brow puckered as she looked over at Honor. "What else?"

"A shower curtain, a bathmat, a new cover for the bed,

and a matching rug." His eyes crinkled in the corners with laughter. "Maybe we should have rented a U-Haul."

"Well." Callie shrugged her shoulders and picked a piece of fuzz off her blue jeans. "You said we could fix up your place." Her eyes narrowed, and she looked over at Honor. "But you are sure you can afford all of this? I don't want you to do without something or not be able to pay a bill because I wanted to fix up your home."

"No." Honor put the truck in gear. "I promise I will be able to buy my groceries and pay my bills next week. Now, where to next?"

"Lowes or Home Depot, either one." Callie bit her lower lip and rubbed her palms together. "We have to pick out a rug for your living room and get a welcome mat for your front door. We don't have to do it today, but we need to eventually get a front porch swing." Callie paused and looked over at Honor.

Honor's eyebrows raised, and he tried to look serious, but his face broke into a smile. "You are really enjoying this."

"I am." Callie leaned over and impulsively laid her head on Honor's shoulder and squeezed his arm. "I've never been able to do anything like this before, you know? Like fix up my own place."

A surge of heat flushed Honor's skin at Callie's touch, the same way it had earlier when he had kept her from falling. His heart beat faster as she continued to talk. He swallowed hard, trying to keep his mind on what she was saying and off of how his body was reacting to her touch, her nearness. "You, uh, haven't fixed up your apartment?" He raised his arm on the steering wheel, and Callie raised her head and sat up. His body immediately reacted in a negative way to her absence. He had to stop himself from pulling her back over next to him—where she had been—where she belonged.

"I've fixed it up, but." Callie reached up and flipped down

her visor and looked at herself in the mirror. "I have not had the... well." She slapped the visor back into place and turned toward Honor as he pulled out of the parking lot into the flow of traffic. "Honestly, this is the first job I've ever had where I could actually afford to buy anything new or even halfway nice."

"That's not surprising." Honor glanced at her nervous expression and then turned his eyes back to the road. "You just finished your first two years of college. You can't work full time and go to school full time and save for the future and furnish a home too. Some things have to be put off until later. I'm sure you had your hands full with school and maybe a part-time job."

"Actually." Callie twisted in the truck seat to where she was facing Honor. "I didn't do a whole lot of work while I was in school. I sort of bummed off my sister and her rich husband."

Honor felt Callie's eyes searching his face. "Well." He paused as he stopped at a red light, thinking about what she had said. "You were young, and you are the baby in the family." He glanced over at her face, anxiety over what she was telling him showing in her eyes. "Everybody needs help when they are starting out. I'm sure they were glad to help you. Besides, now you are working and on your own, right?"

"Right." Callie twisted back around and leaned forward, grabbing her purse.

What was she so nervous about? "Callie." Honor hit his turn signal and pulled into the parking lot of Lowes. The fall sunshine glistened off of the trucks littering the parking lot. Honor eased down an aisle and pulled into a parking spot in front of a display of pumpkins, hay bales and mums. "I can tell you are nervous about something. Maybe about not having a marketing degree, or being young and having this position in my company, or, I don't know, not having a big bank account yet." He pushed the gearshift into park and turned to face her. "You are doing a fantastic job. Hiring you was a great decision, believe me. Clutch reminds me of that often."

"Really?" Callie's mouth turned up at the corners and she looked down, unbuckling her seat belt.

"Yes, really." Honor leaned over and stuck his hand under her chin and tilted her face up. "So, whatever is bothering you, let it go. You deserve to have this job. You are making my company—and my life better. We are friends, remember?"

"Thank you, Honor."

"Now." Honor swallowed. The look in Callie's eyes, the tone of her voice, made his entire body fight against him. He wanted to reach over and pull her to him, hold her close. He pulled his eyes away from her face and unbuckled his seat belt, his fingers trembling slightly from touching her face. "Let's see about that rug."

ould he understand if I told him about Dawson? About the baby? About losing the baby? A sliver of fear ran up Callie's neck as she slid out of the truck and shut the door. He probably would. He was Duck, after all. But was he? Now he was Honor Jacobs, owner of his own company, his own home, her boss. If he didn't understand, and decided she was foolish and thoughtless and childish and a....

Callie followed Honor through the automatic doors and watched as he pulled an industrial sized shopping cart from the rack. A coward. That's what she had been. That's what she was still being, but now was different. She wasn't bumming off of her sister anymore. Well, Fiona was doing her laundry for her today, but she would pay her back with free babysitting. That's how they did things. That wasn't bumming. Now she was working and paying her own way. She hadn't borrowed a single penny from Fiona and Langston since starting this job and had even turned down the gas money Langston had offered her.

She was definitely doing better, being more mature. Telling Honor about *that* shouldn't even be on her radar. It was in the past, and he didn't have any reason to know about it. They were friends, like he said, but not all friends shared everything, especially something she had not even told her sister. Not telling him was not being a coward. She was over-thinking all of this.

What was all this touchy-feely stuff, anyway? Laying her head on his shoulder, over-reacting when he grabbed her this morning. This was not how Callie Madison behaved around a man. Even Dawson hadn't made her behave the way she had been acting lately, and she had really had a thing for Dawson. Even though now she regretted that thing with every fiber of her being.

She adjusted her purse on her shoulder and put a perky smile on her face as they started to the back of the store where the rugs were. "You are going to love your home when we get through with it. Just wait." She looked over at Honor and winked. "You might even be doing one of those parties at your place by Christmas."

"I doubt that." Honor turned down the aisle where the rugs hung one after another from a vertically shaped rack. Rugs of all textures, designs, and colors, hung one after another in rows in front of them. He reached up and ran his fingers through a plushy white shag rug. "Can't get this one. I might never leave home if I put this thing on my floors. Feel this."

"I wouldn't ever put my shoes on. That does feel good."

Callie flipped past the shag rug, passing several that would not do for one reason or another. "How about this one?" She pushed on the hanging hinge so that the rug was more visible. The smoky grey-blue rug with a large white medallion pattern and short pile would look great in his living room. "I think this is it."

"Sure, I mean, it would look better if it was shag." Honor rubbed his hand across his jawline and winked at Callie. "But I guess it will do." He looked down at the rolled up rugs shrink-wrapped in plastic in various sizes that matched the display and found the one he needed. He drug it from the pile and put it in the buggy, the end towering above their heads. "While we are here, why don't we get a couple of lamps, one for the living room and one for the bedroom?"

"Now you're getting in the spirit of things."

They picked out the lamps, checked out, and headed to the truck. The sun was setting, and the streetlights were turning on in the parking lot. "We'd better hurry if we are going to pick out a mattress," Honor said, stopping the buggy at the truck. "We will have to plan another day to put all of this in the house. It's getting late."

"Aww." Callie watched as Honor loaded their latest finds into the back of the truck. "I want to keep working on your house. Let's shop for my mattress another day. I'd rather get back and get all of this set up tonight."

"Are you sure? That means you'll have to sleep on that futon at least another week."

"I'm sure. Besides, we don't want to leave your rug and lamps unattended in the back of the truck while we are in the store. This isn't Carson's Bayou." Callie watched Honor walk around to the other side of the truck as she opened her door. "My back is used to the futon. A few more days won't hurt."

"Alright. Whatever my lady desires." Honor slid onto his seat and started the ignition. "Home it is."

"I'll call a to-go order in to Gumbo Hut for us. We can eat dinner, then get to work."

"Sounds like a plan." Honor buckled the seatbelt and pulled out of the parking lot. "Back to Carson's Bayou, and back to work."

And back to not spilling my guts to my boss. Callie watched Honor out of the corner of her eye as he changed lanes and started toward home. *Sweet Duck. You deserve a nice home and a nice girl. Someone with as good of a heart as you have.*

CHAPTER FOURTEEN

*C*allie lay on her back and moved her arms and legs across the new floor rug in a snow angel pattern. "I think if you fire me, I will move to New York and become an interior designer," she called out to Honor, who was pouring their third cups of coffee for the night. Actually, it was morning since midnight had passed two hours ago. "This was so much fun, and you have to admit that your place looks great."

"I have no trouble admitting that everything looks one hundred percent better." Honor walked up to where Callie was laying and stared down at her, a cup of coffee in each hand. "Should I come down, or are you coming up?"

"Put the coffee down, and come test out your new rug." Callie put her arms out to the side and stretched like a cat waking up from a nap. "I think your floor is a little more comfortable than my futon."

"Well, you might as well grab one of these fancy throw pillows off the couch and stay the night." He placed the coffee on the end table and sat down beside her. "Scoot over. I want to spread out and get the feel of this thing, too." He waited while Callie moved over, then he lay back, spread-eagle on the rug, and stared up at the ceiling. "It's not shag, but it'll do."

"We have to move the coffee table back in place to see how it looks, but it's kind of tempting to leave it like this." Callie rolled over on her side and looked at Honor. "So we can stretch out down here and chat every time I come to visit."

"Who needs a coffee table?" Honor rolled over toward Callie and propped up on his elbow. "I hear they are highly over-rated."

Callie rolled onto her back and looked up at the light fixture. "You need to wash that thing. I see a couple of dead horseflies trapped in the glass."

"Yeah." Honor turned his head and glanced up at the light, but turned back to stare at Callie. "I'll put it on the list." He reached over and brushed a wayward strand of blond hair from her cheek. "This really does mean a lot to me. Even if I had ever gotten around to emptying all my boxes, I never would have gotten my house to look like this. Now I can invite Mrs. Albertson or Lucas and Vivian or anybody else in and not be embarrassed by how everything looks."

"You? Embarrassed?" Callie turned and looked at Honor. "I'm surprised. You never act like anything embarrasses you."

"Still waters run deep." Honor pushed up into a sitting position and reached over to get his cup of coffee. "Under all these layers of manliness lies a beating heart."

"Oh, well." Callie sat up and waited for Honor to hand her a cup of coffee. "Since you put it that way, it makes sense." She took the coffee from his hands and ignored the uptake of her pulse as their fingers brushed together. "You are, after all, the most manly Duck I've ever seen."

"That's right." Honor raised his coffee to his lips and blew the steam from the mug. "And don't you forget it." He took a sip of the scorching liquid as his eyes roamed the room, satisfaction written on his face. "Seriously though, the preacher came by in the summer when the living room was full of boxes. I stepped outside, and we talked on the front porch the whole time. I might invite him and his family over now for something." He turned and looked back at Callie, his eyes squinting in indecision. "Do people still invite people over for coffee, or did that go out with the Brady Bunch?"

"They would probably love it if you invited them over for coffee. Get a cake or something sweet to serve, and have them come over one Sunday afternoon. Of course, since you are staying up all night, you will probably be napping after church today. Make it a Sunday when you are well rested."

"True." Honor's mouth stretched into a yawn, and he turned and put the cup back on the end table. "You really can stay the night if you want to. I can sleep on the couch, and you can have my bed. It's a little late to be driving home."

"Naa." Callie handed Honor her coffee mug and rubbed her eyes, fighting the yawn that was trying to take over. "I'd better head home. Don't want your neighbors getting the wrong idea about us when they wake up and see my car still in front of your house in the morning."

"Are you sure you will be alright going home this late?"

"You forget." Callie stood and reached her hands down to pull Honor up. "It's Carson's Bayou, not a Houston suburb. Unless I happen to hit a deer or start texting and don't pay attention to where I'm going, I will make it home fine. The streets still roll up around here at ten, for the most part."

Honor took her hands, and she leaned back, pulling him to his feet. He held her hands for a couple of seconds too long and smiled as her cheeks turned pink. "You are pretty strong for your size."

"And you are heavier than you look." Callie eased her hands from Honors and rubbed her palms together, attempting to ignore the tingle running up her arms from his touch. "I guess I'll see you Monday morning."

"Sure." Honor clapped his hands in front of him and nodded. "Um. I may call you after church tomorrow, or later today, I guess. You can come see what everything looks like after a good night's sleep. Some things might need some tweaking—or something. I can come pick you up if you are too tired to drive."

"Okay." Callie looked at the sort of dopey expression on Honor's face and laughed. "That will be fine, Duck. If I don't answer right away, just text me, and I'll call you back. I may sleep in."

Callie said goodbye and hurried to her car. The night air was getting a little nippy. It might be a cool Thanksgiving after all, if tonight's weather was any indication of things to come. She waved at Honor, propped in his door frame, as she drove away. Maybe he didn't need to date anybody else. If she really tried, she could be the girl he needed, the girl he deserved. She didn't want to be the impulsive, flighty Callie that she was in college. Yes, she had been a little spoiled, too, but she was changing.

She made it across town to the studio apartment above her brother's garage without any issues, like she knew she would. The house key, cool to the touch, slipped into the locked door at the top of the stairs. She looked down the metal stairs running up the side of the garage and pulled out her phone as she propped in the doorway. A puff of wind blew a swirl of leaves down the steps at her feet as she typed in the text and sent it to Honor. *I made it home. Just letting you know. Goodnight.*

Goodnight. Enjoyed the day.

Callie stepped into her apartment as a car engine roared to life and rolled down the street past the garage. Dawson? She turned her ear toward the sound as she eased the door to. It sounded like his supped-up car. This was getting ridiculous. She was going to have to talk with him and put a stop to his stalking. She peaked out the curtains and down onto the street below. The car had disappeared, and everything was quiet. Maybe it wasn't him. Maybe she was just being paranoid.

onor stifled a yawn as he pulled his car into the gas station after church that afternoon. He had made it to preaching on coffee and sheer willpower. Clutch had ribbed him about missing Sunday school and joked about him keeping late hours, but Honor had refused to tell him anything about his evening. It looked like Clutch hadn't gone anywhere in his Subaru since their swap yesterday. The car was on an eighth of a tank of gas when he left it with his best friend, and it was still there today.

He grabbed the empty Styrofoam coffee cup from the holder and got out of the car. Callie must have left it there when they drove over to get Clutch's truck. He tossed the cup in the trash and opened his gas tank. He put his debit card information into the pump, then put the nozzle in the tank on autopilot as his mind replayed everything that had happened yesterday and last night. Spending time with Callie was becoming a priority. He knew he had that lovesick puppy look on his face last night when she pulled him up from the floor, but he couldn't help it. His logical side was doing battle with his heart, his lovesick lonely heart, and the logical side was getting whipped.

Callie only saw him as her childhood friend or, worse yet, her boss. Would he be able to change her mind where she would see him as dateable boyfriend material? Not some project that she was trying to hook up with the local good girl waitress? Not that there was anything wrong with Elda. She was nice enough and could sing like an angel, but she wasn't Callie. That was the thing. Nobody was going to measure up to Callie. It had become clear to him as he daydreamed his way through the church service that he had two options. He could either try to make Callie see him as more than her friend, or he could go back to focusing on business, push his feelings for her down out of the way.

"Callie sure was late getting home last night."

Honor looked up from where he was pumping gas, the words of the man's voice pulling him out of his internal debate. "Were you following her again?" The nozzle clicked in Honor's hand and he let off of the lever but didn't take it from the gas tank. "You know there are laws against stalking people."

"She never minded me *stalking* her before." Dawson Wallace leaned against the bumper of Honor's car; his lips turned up in a smirk. "As a matter of fact, she didn't mind me doing a lot of things before."

"I'm not going to talk about Callie." The smell of stale beer rolled off of Dawson as he stood there, grinning like an idiot. Honor stepped back, pulling the nozzle from his gas tank. "Especially not with you."

"She's not who you think she is, you know." Dawson leaned closer, his bloodshot eyes glaring at Honor. "Since you moved here and gave her that job, she's suddenly gotten all hoity-toity, but she can't fool me. I know the real Callie and what the real Callie wants."

"You're drunk." Honor tore the receipt for his gas from the pump and stared at the man, unsure what to do. He didn't need to be driving, but the guy certainly wasn't going to take any help from him. He looked past him to the storefront. Dawson's Mustang was pulled in sideways, taking up three parking spots. "You don't need to be behind the wheel."

"Don't worry about me." Dawson laughed, a humorless sound. "I bet she didn't tell you she was pregnant with my kid, did she?" He slapped the trunk of the car with the palm of his hand and grinned as Honor's face transformed into a serious look of concern. "No, I didn't figure she would mention that to her precious Duck."

"What are you talking about?" Honor stepped around the vehicle in front of Dawson. "Callie has a child?"

"No, at least, not anymore. See." Dawson leaned back further against the trunk of the Subaru and propped up on his elbows. "She came to me last year at the end of our third semester and said she was pregnant with my baby. It could have been mine. I mean, she is fine-looking and, well." Dawson let the words trail away.

"Shut-up." Honor leaned in and grabbed the collar of Dawson's shirt.

"See." Dawson laughed, his sour alcohol breath blowing in Honor's face. "I told you she's not who you think she is. She wanted me to give her money for an abortion, but I wasn't raised that way."

Honor pushed Dawson away, releasing his collar. "I don't believe you."

"It's true. I've tried to forget about it, but that was my kid. I think I have a right to," he paused and grinned, an evil glint in his eyes. "Well, I have a right to whatever she's offering since she took my kid from me."

"Get away from me." Honor's voice was low, growling. He no longer cared if the man was capable of driving. It was not his problem. He pushed around Dawson toward his car door.

Dawson stumbled, then laughed again as he regained his footing. "That kind of changes things, doesn't it, *Duck*? She's not the sweet little thing you left behind. I used to get so sick of her comparing everything I said or did to her old friend Duck." He shook a finger toward Honor as he got into his car. "She's not for you, man. The sooner you see that and send her back to me, the better off she will be. I have what she wants, not you."

CHAPTER FIFTEEN

*H*onor didn't look back as he drove away from the gas station. It couldn't be true. Callie wouldn't take the life of her child. She wasn't like that. She couldn't be. He scraped his hand across his face, trying to blot out the picture of Dawson Wallace laughing at him as he talked about Callie aborting her baby.

Where was he going? Honor looked out the windshield, trying to figure out where he was. This wasn't the way home. Where was he? He slowed his car and looked out the side window at the small unkept yards and trailers blended between the empty overgrown lots. He was headed to the other side of town, the area where Sidney Madison's garage was, the garage with the apartment above it where Callie lived.

He pulled into the driveway of what looked like an abandoned house and turned his car around. He needed to go home and cool down, think about what Dawson Wallace had told him. Really, he should laugh this entire thing away. The man was drunk and obviously obsessed with Callie. He would probably say anything to manipulate the situation in his favor.

The car drove back across town toward his home as Honor's thoughts darted one way and then another, refusing to calm down. Callie had never denied that Dawson had been her boyfriend. Of course, they had never really talked much about her life during the time he was away. Why was that? Why did she always turn the subject back to him?

He pulled up to his house and walked to his front door, suddenly exhausted, his legs feeling like they were full of iron. His phone vibrated as he unlocked his front door and stepped inside. *Are we still on for this afternoon? I can pick up chicken and dumplings from the grocery store deli for dinner if you want.*

Honor stared at his phone for a few seconds before a wave of anger washed over him. He hurled the phone across the room, and it landed on the sofa with a thud. He ran his hands across the sides of his scalp and squeezed, trying to mesh the Callie Dawson Wallace had described with the Callie that was here the day before, laughing at pictures of him as a kid, talking about her family and nieces, helping him get his life together.

He stumbled over to the sofa and fell onto the cushions, picking up the phone. He started typing a response several times, but always backed it out, not knowing what to say.

Duck. You okay?

Honor held the buttons on the side of the phone until it turned off. He couldn't see her right now, not until he got his act together. He didn't know if what her old boyfriend said was true, false, or somewhere in between. How could he find out? The only sure way was to ask Callie. She was a smooth talker, but he could tell when she was lying. She knew he could tell so she would often beat around the bush, but ended up telling him the truth. They had been that way since they were young.

What if it was true? Was he ready to hear that? Her child dead, for what reason? Did it matter? He leaned forward and put his head in the palms of his hands. He was falling in love with her, was already in love with her, if he was honest with himself. Could he love a woman that would put her wants above the life of her child? He raised his head and looked around the room, every part of it reminding him of Callie. A Callie who was caring and loving and helpful. He stretched out on the couch and stared up at the ceiling, at the light fixture with the dead horseflies in the glass. Maybe she had been with a few other guys. The idea made his gut burn, but if he loved her, he couldn't hold that against her. If they started dating, she would be faithful to him. She was that type of person.

Could he forgive her for the… he couldn't even finish the thought. He closed his eyes, wanting to go back to this morning, before the gas station, before Dawson Wallace had ruined his world. One thing was certain. He couldn't move forward with his plans to pursue Callie until he had this settled in his mind and his heart. He would eventually have to talk to her about all of this, find out what really happened, find out if she was a Christian. He assumed she was. She had gone to church when they were young, and he assumed she still went to the enormous church in town with her sister and brother. His mind drifted into sleep as scenes of Callie from the past mingled with the ones from the present. He had assumed a lot of things—too many things.

"Honor." Callie stepped into the little office with the bare walls and looked down at her friend. "What gives? You never got back with me yesterday, and you're still not answering your phone."

She tapped the toe of her high heel shoe against the floor; the sound reverberating in the small space. "Honor?" She stared at his down-turned head, ignoring her as he frowned into his computer screen. She put her hands on her hips and tilted her head to the side. "Hello. I'm waiting for an answer."

"I was tired." Honor continued to look at the computer screen, his voice monotone, dismissive.

"Okay. I get that." Callie stepped closer to his desk and leaned forward into his personal space. "So was I, but when you say you are going to call a girl, it's rude to not call her. It's even worse when the girl tries to call you, and you don't have the courtesy to pick up your phone or return a text."

"Let it go, Callie." Honor typed something on the keyboard and moved the mouse. "I'm busy right now."

"Well, heaven forbid I mess up your schedule." Callie knew her voice was too loud, that she was not being professional, but where did he get off acting like a jerk? "I'm going to go back to my office and wait until you have time for me if that's okay with you, Mr. Jacobs." She frowned down at the top of his head. "At least look at me when you dismiss me."

Honor raised his head. "Clutch is going with you today to talk to the school in Shreveport. I've got some things to take care of." His eyes, red-rimmed and hollow with dark circles, stared into hers. "Unless you have something very important to tell me, I would appreciate being left alone until you leave."

"Duck." Callie's eyes softened with compassion, the anger from seconds before gone. "Are you okay? You look awful."

"I'm fine." Honor leaned back in the chair, his shoulders slumped. "Shut the door on your way out."

Callie walked out of the office and up the hall, her forehead wrinkled. What was going on? She walked into the break room and slouched into the chair. Duck had never acted that way before. He had never dismissed her like she didn't matter. Her mind went over everything they had done together on Saturday, and then to the party the night before. Was he tired of her pushiness? She had kind of taken over his house, but he had seemed to be happy with that. Had he noticed how Dawson was hanging around the office? Was Dawson showing up at their church party the last straw for Honor? No. Honor wasn't like that. He wouldn't turn on her because of the way someone else was acting.

"Hey." Clutch stuck his head through the doorway and smiled at Callie. "You about ready to go? We need to leave in a few minutes if we want to make it to Shreveport in time for the meeting."

"Yeah." Callie stood up from the chair and tugged down on her gray tweed skirt. "Clutch." Callie looked over at the Clark Kent look-alike in his black suit and yellow tie. "You have on your suit, so you must have known you were going with me today instead of Honor."

"He called me last night and told me he needed me to take over on the presentations for a while. He needed a change of pace."

"Has he ever done that before?" Callie stepped over to the doorway. "Asked you to fill in for him like this?" *A while? How long is he going to avoid me?*

"Before you came along, he and I went together on these trips, so don't worry, I know what I'm doing." Clutch's smile faded as he looked at Callie's serious expression. "What's wrong, Callie?"

"I don't know." Callie forced her lips up into a smile. "Nothing, I guess."

"Are you sure?" Clutch followed Callie to her desk and waited while she retrieved her purse. "You look like you are upset about something."

"Have you talked to Honor this morning? He seems. I don't know." Callie shrugged her shoulders. She didn't want Clutch to know how Honor had acted a few minutes ago, how he had brushed her off, dismissed her. "Do you think he may be getting sick or something?"

"Honor? He never gets sick. Na." Clutch held open the office door, and Callie stepped out into the crisp November air. "He looked tired this morning, but he said you two stayed up all night Saturday night fixing up his house. Honor is a real homebody. It's probably taking him a couple of days to recover from not getting any sleep that night."

"I guess." Callie followed Clutch to his truck and slid into the passenger's seat. She looked across the street and breathed a sigh of relief. At least Dawson wasn't hanging out at her car this morning, although it was still a little early for him to be out and about. She definitely had to call him soon and set some boundaries. If he got her fired from this job, she would skin his hide.

"Honor said his house looks great."

"You think he really likes it?" Callie buckled her seatbelt and looked over at Clutch. "He's not mad at me for pushing him into redoing everything?"

"Are you kidding?" Clutch chuckled as he looked in his rearview mirror. "If Honor had not wanted you to help him do that, he would have told you. He's not big on beating around the bush."

"No. Guess not."

"He thinks you did a great job." Clutch pulled out onto the street and headed out of town. "From what I can tell, he thinks you are doing great all around. Relax, Callie. He's just tired. He'll be back to his bossy self by tomorrow, or the next day at the latest."

Callie smiled, but kept her doubts to herself. Something was going on with Honor. She could tell, even if Clutch couldn't.

CHAPTER SIXTEEN

"What's wrong with you?" Fiona handed Callie a glass of Dr. Pepper, then sat down on the couch next to her little sister. "You've been moping around all week and acting like you've lost your best friend."

Callie took a long sip from the straw and swallowed, not sure how to answer. "It's complicated." She had come over that Saturday morning, as usual, to do her laundry, but instead of dropping it off for Fiona to take care of so she could go about her business, she had collapsed on the leather sofa, exhausted from the emotional rollercoaster her life had become.

"Complicated my eye. It's me, your sister. What's happened to get you so down in the mouth?" Fiona took a swallow of her orange juice and frowned. "You haven't lost your job, have you? I thought you were doing well there."

"I was, I mean I am." She took another pull from the straw and set the glass on the coffee table. "Things were going great. Honor and I were seeing the clients and working so well together, but all of the sudden something happened."

"Like what?" Fiona took another sip of the orange juice. "Did you mess something up?"

"No." Callie's brow lowered over her eyes. "At least I don't think I did. Monday when I got to the office Honor looked like death warmed over. He wouldn't talk to me. He wouldn't even fight with me." She leaned back and pulled her knees into her chest, her flannel pajama bottoms snuggling against her arms. "Ever since then, he's barely mumbled two words to me, and Clutch has taken over going to do the presentations. I can't decide if he's avoiding me personally or if there is something wrong with how I'm working or if there is something going on with him that he doesn't want to share with me."

"He looked sick the day all of this started?" Fiona leaned forward and set her glass on a coaster on the coffee table. She slid a coaster under Callie's glass, then leaned back on the couch.

"Yeah, he did." Callie's eyes narrowed as a hint of fear crept into her voice. "Fi, you don't think Honor's sick or something like that, do you? I mean, like really sick? We are best friends. Undoubtably, he would tell me if he had some kind of serious illness."

"Don't jump to conclusions." Fiona threw a lock of chestnut curls over her shoulder. "He's probably got something going on with his dad or with the business that has him distracted." She reached over and patted her sister's arm. "It's going to be okay. He probably needs a little space. I mean, I know you are friends, but he was away for a long time. Things change. Both of you have probably changed a lot since you were best friends, right? Like when you were back in school? It's probably something private. Give him time. He will come around."

Fiona scooted closer to her little sister. "Hey, you want to see something that will cheer you up?"

"Yeah." Callie sighed and forced a smile onto her face. "I guess so."

Fiona slipped her hand into a pocket of her willowy skirt and pulled out what looked like a polaroid picture. "Want to see the first picture of little baby Wade? His daddy hasn't even seen him yet."

Callie felt her color drain away as she looked down at the little face, the closed eyes, the nose and lips mushed against its mother's tummy. Even though no one could tell yet, the tiny baby was growing inside her sister. Even while they were sitting there on the couch talking about Callie's problems, her sister's baby was there too, secure, knowing his mother would protect him and care for him.

"Oh, Fiona." Callie drug in a deep breath and tried to control the sob starting down in her chest. "I did something awful. I did something awful, and God took someone from me." Her chest heaved as she cried out the last words. "I was pregnant, and I didn't want the baby, and I." Callie sobbed the words into Fiona's shoulder. Blond curls tumbled over her face as the sonogram picture slipped from her fingers onto the couch.

"Hey, hey, hey." Fiona wrapped her arms around Callie's shoulders and started stroking her head. "It's okay, honey. Take a deep breath before you hyperventilate." Fiona continued to stroke Callie's head until the sobbing slowed. "Here." She picked up the glass of Dr. Pepper. "Take a sip of this, and see if you can tell me what happened."

Callie sniffed and wiped her nose on the paper towel that had been wrapped around the glass. She took a drink of the soda and let out a ragged breath. "You may hate me after I tell you what I did."

"I'm not going to hate you." Fiona wiped a tear off Callie's cheek with her thumb. "I may not agree with what you did, and you know if I don't, I will tell you. But sweetie." Fiona paused and lifted Callie's down-turned face. "You're the only sister I have. I will always love you."

"Well, remember back when I dropped out of volleyball and debate team toward the end of my second semester?"

"Yeah. When you started going hog wild?"

"Yeah. I guess that's one way to put it." Callie sniffed again and wiped her nose. "I had started dating Dawson Wallace a little before that, but I kept it a secret because I knew you and Sid didn't like him."

"Sid and I figured that's what was going on."

Callie looked up at Fiona, then back at the paper towel in her hands. "Well." She pulled in a breath of air and blew it out. "By the time I figured I had better tell you and Sid about dating him... before somebody else told you, we were already." She paused and swallowed the lump in her throat.

"You were already fooling around?"

"Yeah. All the time."

"I imagined that's what was going on. I should have asked you about it. I knew you were doing something you shouldn't have been doing, and I looked the other way. That was wrong. You're my little sister. You deserve better from me." Fiona leaned over and picked up her orange juice. She took a drink while Callie wiped her nose again. "I never understood what you saw in that guy, Cal. I guess all that's neither here nor there now." She sat the glass down and leaned back on the couch. "So, what happened?"

"About this time last year, a little before Thanksgiving, I missed a period. I freaked out. You know I'm as regular as a clock."

"You were pregnant?" Fiona's voice was quiet. She watched Callie, her face masked in calmness.

"Yes." Callie looked up at her sister, and tears welled up in her eyes again. "At least I believed I was. I told Dawson, and he said he could get in touch with a doctor to get rid of it. I mean, get rid of my baby."

"Did you have an abortion?"

"No." Callie's eyes searched her sister's face. "No. Fi, you know me better than that. I'm loud and selfish and tell lies and I'm lazy, but I would never harm a baby." She blinked back the tears, her voice begging her sister. "You believe me, don't you?"

"Of course I believe you." Fiona nodded, tears forming in her own eyes, relief in her voice. "What happened? Is that when you started buckling down with your classes again?"

"Yeah." Callie swallowed, her throat tight with emotion. "I broke up with Dawson as soon as he said that, but then," Callie paused, a sob catching in her throat. "In February, when I would have been three months pregnant, I had a really horrible period."

"You lost the baby?"

"I guess so." Callie's breath shuddered. "I must have."

"But you never got a pregnancy test?" Fiona's brow pulled together in confusion. "You never went to a doctor?"

"No." Callie's eyes stretched wide like saucers as she looked at her sister. "I wanted to, but you know what would have happened if I had bought a pregnancy test at the dollar store or Target. Everybody in town would have found out about my business. I couldn't handle dealing with all that. It was stupid, but it's what happened."

"But Callie. You don't even know for sure that you were pregnant."

"I was, Fi." Callie raked her hand across her cheek, swiping away a tear. "I know I had to be, and then I lost the baby. I didn't want the baby, and then I lost the baby."

"No." Fiona shook her head and took both of Callie's hands into hers. "It doesn't work that way, Callie, and you know it. You don't lose a baby because you don't want the baby. Me or you or Sid wouldn't be alive today if that were the case, and you know it."

"But."

"No, Cal. Listen to me. If you were pregnant and lost the baby, it did not happen because you didn't want it. It just happened. Miscarriages happen because they happen, not because of something going on in your head."

"I only didn't want it for a while. After the shock wore off, I made up my mind that there was no way around it. I decided I would make the best of it. After that I was kind of, I don't know." Callie's eyes looked over to the baby monitor on the mantel above the fireplace, then down at the tiny face on the picture between her and Fiona. "I was kind of happy to have someone to love, who would love me, the real me." She turned her eyes back to her sister. "I guess it is silly, but when I started bleeding, I wanted to roll over and die. I felt like God was taking the baby away because I didn't deserve it."

"Come here." Fiona leaned over and wrapped her arms around her sister again, pulling her in close. "You know how much I love you, right?" She waited while Callie's head bobbed up and down against her shoulder. "You have to understand that God loves you even more than I do."

"I don't understand how he could, Fi. I'm not a good person like you."

"Ha." Fiona leaned her head back and let out a bark of laughter. "You have got to be kidding me. You know how my temper is, how prideful I am, how I can hold a grudge." She leaned back and looked into her little sister's face. "Nobody is good enough to deserve God's love. That's what makes God so marvelous. He loved us even when we were unlovable, Sis. Not just me, but everyone else who has given their lives to him. It's called grace. He loves us even when we don't deserve it."

"How do I get him to love me like that?" Callie's lower lip

trembled. "I want God to love me. I can't do this anymore without him. I'm all done in."

"He already loves you. You have to accept his love. Give your life to him, and love him back. That's what He wants. He doesn't want to punish you for things you did before you knew him. He wants you to turn to him, ask forgiveness for all that stuff in the past, and love him in return."

"Help me pray, Fi. I need to tell God all this—stuff. Tell him about the mess I made, get it all right. I can't make it through if I don't get it right with God."

"I will." Tears caused Fiona's voice to sound clogged, but the look of joy on her face let Callie know she was ecstatic with the choice she was making.

After she prayed, a peace settled in Callie's mind that had been missing. She still didn't understand what was going on with Honor. It still hurt terribly to think he was pulling away from her, but at least now she knew that wherever she was, she was not alone. She did not have to figure everything out on her own today or ever again.

Now that she and Fiona had talked things out, she also knew her sister would be in her corner no matter what happened. If, for some reason, Honor decided to let her go, she would find another job, even work at the snow cone stand. That didn't matter. What mattered was finding out what was going on with him. Why was he pushing her away, shutting her out? She needed to see him, force him to talk. Go sit on top of his desk and refuse to move, if that is what it took. She loved him too much...

She leaned her eyes back and stared at the ceiling as the realization of what she told herself slammed into her brain. She loved him. She loved Honor Jacobs, but as a friend, surely only as a friend, like she had ever since she could remember.

No. Clutch was her friend. When he had held her hand to

step over a giant puddle in the parking lot of a high school after a presentation on Tuesday, her heart didn't do flip-flops like it did with Honor. She thought about kissing Clutch, and a faint queasiness formed in her gut. He was not Honor, and it wouldn't be right.

No, Clutch was only a friend. Honor was more. Now, she had to figure out a way to find out how much more, and if it even mattered. If Honor didn't want her around, what did it matter how she felt?

CHAPTER SEVENTEEN

*C*allie pulled into the church parking lot and looked at the cars of different sizes and price points scattered about the lot. Her old clunker, well Fiona's old clunker, blended well with the mix of vehicles. Everything from newer model Mercedes to ancient looking pickups as well as everything in between were parked all around her.

Two stained glass windows, each a mixture of deep jewel tones, faced the street on either side of the enormous wooden double doors. Several more windows ran down either side of the white wooden church house. A well cared for flower bed filled with purple ornamental cabbages and pansies in an array of colors lined the front of the covered porch. She stretched her neck up and looked at the steeple towering above with the cross on top. Would these people welcome her in? Everyone had been friendly at the party at Lucas Wade's house, but still, it was a little intimidating to walk inside alone.

This church wasn't nearly as large as the one she had gone to all of her life. She had never missed Sunday school and the worship service as a child, going with Nana and her siblings. Even as a teen, even after Nana had Alzheimer's and was in a home, she still attended church. Nana expected her to go, and she didn't disappoint Nana. After she started college she went less and less. Fiona had pushed her to attend at first, but after a while she stopped prodding her.

After yesterday; however, it was time to start back, to attend for the right reasons, to get to know God better. Yesterday afternoon she had driven back to her apartment and was putting away her laundry when her phone vibrated with a text. *Callie, Elda and I are singing a duet tomorrow at church. I'd really appreciate it if you would come and offer a little moral support.*

At first, Callie was going to decline Clutch's offer. She would attend church with Fiona like she always had. But why not go and support Clutch? This past week they had driven to three different schools to present the software. They had spent hours in his truck where she had picked his brain about Honor, and his time away from Carson's Bayou. Clutch had been great, not pushing her to tell him what was going on, not prying into her reasons for not asking Honor herself about his past. She already knew a few people that went to his church, including Honor. It might be a good idea to make a clean start at a different place. If it didn't work out, she would go to church with Fiona next week.

A peck on her window caused Callie to jump, startling her from her ponderings. A plump, silver-haired lady holding onto a walker smiled at her through the glass. "You getting out, honey?"

Callie smiled and nodded. She watched through the window while the woman moved out of the way, then she opened the door. "This is my first Sunday here," Callie said to the woman as she shut the door and straightened her dress, brushing her fingers over the chocolate colored corduroy. "I was just getting myself together before I walked in."

"Well, we can walk in together, and you can do me a little favor at the same time." The lady pushed her walker forward across the bumpy pavement, and Callie started across the parking lot beside her. "You ready for Thursday, honey?"

"Um." Callie dropped back behind the lady as they made their way through a narrow opening between a couple of cars. "Yes, ma'am. I go to my sister's house for Thanksgiving and help her with the cooking, so there's not a lot for me to do yet." They made it through the bottlenecked area and reached the covered opening to the church doors. "Here. Let me open that for you."

"Thank you, honey." The woman pulled her white cardigan close around her shoulders as she waited for Callie to pull open one of the heavy wooden doors. "They always keep it a tad above freezing in the sanctuary. The preacher says it's easier to pay attention when you aren't too warm." She stepped through the door into the foyer and waited for Callie to walk beside her. "I say it's harder to fall asleep when your teeth are chattering."

Callie smiled at the woman's comment as she peered into the sanctuary, already filling with people of all ages. Some were dressed a little nicer, like she was, wearing one of her work outfits, but most were in their ordinary clothes, jeans and t-shirts, simple dresses, khakis and polos, all smiling and talking with each other as they found a place to sit.

"Come sit by me." The old woman patted Callie's hand. "But first, hand this little package over to that young woman with the red hair sitting a couple of pews down. She gave me a wonderful picture she drew of me sitting on my front porch. I wanted to do something nice for her in return."

"Don't you want to give it to her yourself?" Callie asked, looking at the back of the woman's red head. The woman leaned over to adjust a blanket on a baby carrier sitting beside her. "I'm sure she wants to talk to you."

"No, honey. I need to sit down before these wobbly legs give out. Pushing this walker through that parking lot, then through this carpet, is worse than hoeing a row of corn. You hand her that package, then come sit beside me. I'm so glad I bumped into you. I've been praying that you would come."

Callie's brow rose at the old woman's comment, but she was already turning and walking toward the stained-glass windows to their left. Callie took the little container the old lady had retrieved from the basket on the front of her walker. She stepped over to the woman with the flaming red curls. "Excuse me." She tapped her on the shoulder. The lady turned and smiled up at Callie, her green eyes surprised to see a new face. "The lady with the walker asked me to give these to you." Callie nodded in the old woman's direction. "She needed to go sit down, so I said I would deliver them."

"Oh. I hope it's a batch of her peanut butter cookies," the woman said, her smile growing wider. "My husband and son inhale them when she brings them to things here at the church." She lifted the lid of the container and inhaled, closing her eyes as the aroma of the cookies floated up to her nose. "I may hide these and eat a few on my own before I share."

"They do smell good," Callie said, watching the woman's face. "My name is Callie Madison." She stuck her hand out for the woman to shake. Some of the tension she had felt when she first drove up this morning eased. These people seemed like everyday folks, people she would be friends with.

"Hello, Callie Madison." The redhead popped the container lid shut and reached her hand up. "I'm Darcy Carson. Tell Mrs. Albertson thank you for the cookies and that I will return the container when I'm done. Sometimes I get a chance to talk to her after church, but sometimes I get sidetracked." She nodded down to the sleeping baby with a head full of red curls every bit as bright as her mother's. "People tend to hover around our little Molly."

"I can see why." Callie said, smiling down at the tiny face snuggled under the knitted pink blanket. She said goodbye to the woman and her beautiful baby and turned, looking across the row of pews. Mrs. Albertson. That was the woman who lived across the street from Honor. He had mentioned her a few times back when he was still talking to her... before he shut her out of his life.

Callie sighed. She walked around the edge of the room near the row of stained-glass windows and made her way halfway down the pews where Mrs. Albertson was waiting. She slipped into the open space beside the old woman. "So, you are Honor's neighbor?"

"I am." Mrs. Albertson reached a wrinkled hand up and adjusted her thick glasses. "He's a sweet young man, but I'm afraid he works too hard."

Callie tugged at her fitted dress, making sure the buttons down the front were not puckered, especially across the hips. She crossed her legs and pulled the hem down to right above her knee. "He's my boss," she said, looking at the woman out of the corner of her eye, "but I bet you already know that since you said you were praying for me to come to church."

"Yes, I did." She smiled at Callie, watching her fidget. "I've been waiting for him to bring you himself, but since he hasn't, I'm glad you made it here on your own."

"Does he come here regularly?" Callie's eyes scanned the room. A side door was opening, and a group of elementary kids were filing in, laughing as they made their way to where they would sit.

"He's starting to come pretty often. His friend Clutch never misses." Mrs. Albertson stared at Callie's face as she watched the people coming through the doors. "I'm sure you know Clutch, too. He said he was going to invite you to come today. I can't wait to hear the song he wrote."

"He wrote the song he's singing?" Callie looked at Mrs. Albertson. "He seems to have a lot of hidden talents."

"Not too hidden after today." Mrs. Albertson turned and nodded to another set of doors that opened on the other side of the pulpit. "I believe that's who you are looking for, though."

Callie turned her gaze to where Mrs. Albertson indicated. A look of longing filled her eyes as Honor stepped through the door, smiling and talking with Vivian Wade. He looked like his normal happy self today, not the serious, stern boss he had been all week. Maybe he was only putting on the boss persona when he was around her. She rolled her lips in and looked down at her hands. *I'm not here to see Honor. I'm here to learn about you, God. Help me to not whine my way through church.*

Honor separated from the dark-haired beauty and started walking down the center aisle, stopping to speak to different people in the ever-filling sanctuary as he made his way in their direction. He shook an elderly man's hand and then looked up to where Callie and Mrs. Albertson were sitting. His eyes met Callie's and her lips turned up in a small, hopeful smile. *Please don't shut down. Please be happy to see me.* Honor's eyes narrowed in confusion as his hand came up to stroke his jaw. After a second, the corners of his mouth turned up, and a smile settled on his face.

Mrs. Albertson raised her hand and waved Honor over. "Come sit with me, son. I saved you a spot."

Honor eased down the pew from the other side and sat next to his neighbor. He leaned forward and nodded at Callie. "It's good to see you."

"Clutch invited me," Callie said, smiling across to where he sat staring at her, actually looking at her for the first time since early last Sunday morning. Had Clutch been right? Had he just been tired? "You look well."

"So do you."

Callie waited, hoping he would say more, but he leaned back and looked toward the front, where a man, probably in his mid-thirties, was stepping up to the podium. Callie sat back and listened as the man thanked everyone for coming.

Mrs. Albertson leaned over and whispered in Callie's ear as the man asked everyone to stand for prayer. "Come to my house for dinner after the service, honey. I've invited Honor."

Callie frowned. "I don't know."

"He's pining away like a sick puppy, honey, just like you. Come on over."

Callie swallowed the lump in her throat as she thought about the past week and how miserable she had been since they had quit talking. "Okay," she whispered. *What have I got to lose?*

CHAPTER EIGHTEEN

*S*aying it was a rough week was an understatement. Honor bowed his head as the preacher finished his sermon with the final prayer. Honor had prayed a lot this week. Prayed for Callie, prayed for himself, prayed for clarity, and prayed for wisdom and the right words to say when he talked to her. He assumed when he moved back to town that Callie was the same person she had been when he left. Now he realized how ridiculous that assumption was. He wasn't the same. He left when they were kids, especially her. He had changed, matured, grown. She had too. He assumed she would have grown in the same direction as him. If she had an abortion, then she hadn't.

He wanted to talk to Clutch about it, but Callie hadn't said anything to his friend about her past. It wouldn't be right to tell Clutch what he knew. He had hinted around about it vaguely, without any details on Friday after Callie left.

"I don't know what's going on with you and Callie." Clutch poured the last of the ultra-black coffee that had been brewing all day into his cup. He took a sip. "But whatever it is, you need to work it out. Both of you look like a couple of love-sick hounds. She has moped all week. And you." He smiled and shook his head. "You are hopeless." He leaned against the counter and looked down at Honor sitting at the break room table, his shoulders slumped forward. "She puts on her game face for the presentations and charms the clients like there's nothing to it, but the minute she gets in the truck, she's the female version of the way you are acting right now."

"What if you found out something that totally shattered your perception of who a person was?" Honor fell back in the chair, the weight of Callie's secret wearing him down like a boulder strapped to his shoulders. "What if the person you thought you knew?" Honor rubbed his hand across his grizzly jaw. *Did I shave this morning?* "Had done something that the person you thought you knew would never do?" He turned his eyes away from the ceiling where he was staring and searched Clutch's face. "How would you deal with it?"

"I would talk to her, find out her reasons for doing what she did." Clutch pulled out the other metal chair and sat down. "Whatever it is, ignoring her, treating her like she's not even here will not make things better. Eventually, you're going to drive her away. She's tough, but sooner or later she will cut her losses and move on."

Clutch tilted his head to the side and looked at Honor's face. "Is that what you are wanting? If it is, you are making a mistake. From a business point of view, she's going to be extremely hard to replace. She is hardworking and picked up on our software system just like that. She's outgoing and easy on the eye. She puts people at ease when she talks to them and makes them want to listen to what she's talking about, even our boring product." Clutch leaned back in the chair and stretched his long legs out in front of him. "If that were all there was to it, then I could see letting her walk out of your life, but let's face it. She has you wrapped so tight around her finger." He paused and held up his hand as Honor's head jerked up. "It's as plain as the nose on your face, man. Plain to me because I'm your best friend, but plain to anybody that's around the two of you for more than five minutes. I don't have a clue what she's done, but you are either going to have to forgive her and move on, or cut your losses and let her go, because what you're doing is going to drive her away."

"What if I forgive her?" Honor drew in a breath of air and blew it out slowly. "How can I trust her? What if she decides to do it again?"

"Talk to her, man." Clutch's eyebrows pulled together. "Give her a chance to explain herself. Chances are, you haven't gotten the entire story about whatever it is, and whatever it is can be forgiven. I mean, come on." He sat forward and picked up his coffee mug. "You are supposed to be the hands and feet of Christ. You are in the forgiving business."

"That's another thing. What if she's not a Christian? What if I've fallen for her, and she's not a believer?"

"Talk. To. The. Woman." Clutch drained the last bit of burned coffee from the mug and stood back up. "And don't go at her with a whip and bullhorn assuming you are right and have all the answers. Listen to her." He sat the mug in the sink and turned back to Honor. "Make sure you know what you're talking about, and even if you are right and have all your facts straight, don't forget that your sins nailed Jesus to the cross. That thought should knock you off your high horse and help you get on an even playing field with her, no matter what it is you think she's done."

"Yeah." Honor watched Clutch walk to the door. "You're right. I've got to talk to her."

"Sooner than later, my friend." Clutch stopped in the

doorway. "Another week of working with you two like this, and I'm packing up and going back to Houston."

Honor raised his head as the pastor said amen. Clutch was right. Before he condemned Callie, which was the wrong attitude anyway, he needed to talk to her. He had gone for his daily run yesterday morning and pounded out what he would say to her with every step he made. He ran the trail around the park until his tongue was hanging out, figuring out how to approach her, but had finally given up. This morning, instead of going to Sunday school, he had talked with the pastor and received the same advice from him that he had from Clutch. Talk to Callie with an open mind and an open heart. He was assuming things about a person he said he loved, assuming the worst. The pastor had prayed for him, for Callie, and for their upcoming talk. When he walked into the sanctuary and saw her sitting by Mrs. Albertson, he was sure he was making the right decision. It was time to get things straight.

He would ask her out to lunch, tell her what Dawson Wallace said, and find out what really happened and why. There was absolutely no reason to kill an innocent baby, but he loved her and would not hold her past against her. If she was not a believer, he couldn't expect her to act like she was. As hard as it was going to be, if she was not a believer, he would have to take a step back, not pursue this longing, this passion growing inside of him to be more than friends. Friends would have to be enough.

That thought alone was driving him bonkers. How would he do that? See her every day and stay Honor, the friend. He didn't know, but he would cross that bridge when he got to it —if he got to it. If she was a believer and had done this, well, then he needed to find out the whole story. Find out her reasons and beliefs for doing what she had done, and then decide where to go from there.

Honor followed Mrs. Albertson out of the pew, and they shuffled their way toward the back of the church with the flow of other people laughing and talking as they went. Their progression was extra slow because of everyone speaking to Callie, telling her they were glad she came and hoped she would be back. He watched her laugh and lay her hand on the shoulder of a man her age that they had both known since childhood. A twisting in his gut reminded him he'd pushed her away all week long. He had no claims on her whatsoever. He rubbed his hand across the back of his neck as he watched her lean in and whisper something in the man's ear. The guy wrapped his arms around Callie and pulled her in for a hug as they both laughed some more. The twisting inside him turned a little tighter. He jerked his eyes away, looking anywhere but at the two of them sharing something that he longed to be a part of. He had to get this right with her. Now that he had come out of his week-long pity-party and was ready to act, get things settled, seeing her talk with another man, even a good guy like she was talking to, was torture.

"Don't worry." Mrs. Albertson leaned toward Honor and whispered. The gray-haired lady's walker stood between her and Callie as she stepped back to speak to Honor who was waiting behind her. "She's in love with you, not him."

Honor pulled his eyes away from Callie and looked down at Mrs. Albertson. "Am I that obvious?"

"Yes, you are." Mrs. Albertson reached up and patted his cheek. "She's coming to my house for Sunday dinner. I told her you would be there too."

Callie looked back toward Honor and Mrs. Albertson as she moved forward, away from their friend, and made her way around the last pew. They were on the home stretch to the back door, where the preacher waited to shake their hands. Her eyes caught his, and a look, a new look that

Honor hadn't seen before, made his breath catch in his throat. "I'll be there," he said, not taking his eyes away from the woman he had almost pushed out of his life.

Was there really something new in her expression? Was he seeing things because he wanted to see things? He looked on as she stepped up and the pastor took both of her hands in his. She leaned in again, like she had with the other man, and whispered in the pastor's ear. A huge smile broke out on his face. He pulled her in for a hug, and that same feeling clawed its way back up—jealousy. That's what it was. He was jealous of his pastor, his happily married, completely trustworthy pastor, for hugging Callie. What was she telling these men that made them hug her like that? Why hadn't she told him whatever it was? Had she told Clutch? He looked past the preacher, through the double doors propped wide to let the worshippers flow out more easily to the parking lot outside. Clutch was easy to spot, towering over almost every other person around him. A group of gray-headed women had him pinned up near his truck, and he was patiently nodding his head about whatever they were telling him. No, he wouldn't worry about talking to Clutch right now.

He stepped up to the pastor behind Mrs. Albertson and shook his hand. "Thank you for the talk and prayer this morning. I'm going to do what we planned, probably this afternoon."

"She seems like a very nice girl. I will keep praying that all goes well."

Honor stared at the preacher for another couple of seconds, wanting to ask what Callie had whispered in his ear, but knew it would do no good. "Thank you. I appreciate that."

He followed Mrs. Albertson down the ramp at the side of the covered breezeway, holding her elbow to make sure she didn't stumble on the slight incline leading to the parking lot.

"Let me get that thing of cookies you made for Darcy out of my car, then we can head to your house," Honor said, looking down at the old woman. He looked at Callie, who was waiting at the bottom of the ramp. "It won't take but a moment, then we will head to her house. You can wait and follow us, or we will meet you there."

"We've already delivered the cookies," Mrs. Albertson said, grinning up at Honor. "I think I'm going to ride back with Callie. I've always wanted to ride in one of those little doodlebugs."

"Oh." Honor looked at both women, both staring at him, smiling like a couple of Cheshire cats. "Well. I guess I will see you there."

CHAPTER NINETEEN

*C*allie dabbed the napkin to her lips and leaned back in her chair. "I believe that is the best roast I've had since Nana died." She looked at Mrs. Alberton, beaming at the compliment. "I don't see how you get up and get everything done before going to Sunday school. I was running around like a chicken with my head cut off trying to get myself to worship service. If you hadn't invited me here, I would have probably eaten a bowl of ice cream for lunch."

"I've had years of practice." Mrs. Albertson pinched off a corner of her roll and dropped it in the rich brown gravy pooling around the last piece of potato on her plate. "Planning ahead is the key, and this is an easy meal to fix for Sunday. I could probably do it in my sleep."

"Easy for you," Callie laughed, raising an eyebrow. "I'll never learn to cook like this."

"Wait until you taste the banana pudding," Honor said, watching Callie from across the little dining room table. "It is one of the best things I've ever eaten."

"Oh, hush." Mrs. Albertson picked up the piece of roll

with her fork, the gravy dripping down onto her plate. "You are going to make me blush, son."

"It's true." Honor winked at Callie. "I don't know what you put in there, but I've never had a banana taste that good before."

Callie laid her napkin beside her plate and picked up her almost empty tea glass. "I can't wait. Banana pudding is another one of my favorites."

"Why don't we clear the table and straighten up the kitchen?" Honor started stacking empty dishes on his cleaned plate. "You go sit down and put your feet up, Mrs. Albertson. We'll bring you a bowl of pudding when we're done."

"You are my guests. You shouldn't have to do all that." A glimmer of mischief sparkled in Mrs. Albertson's eyes. "But I am a little tired. I believe I'll take you up on the offer." She laid her napkin on the table and pushed back her chair. "Turn on the coffee pot. It's ready to go and will be a nice pick-me-up to go with our dessert."

Honor stood and gathered Callie's and Mrs. Albertson's plates. "That's an excellent motivator to get this little job done in a hurry. I'll have your dishes washed in no time flat."

Callie pushed back her chair. "Let me help Mrs. Albertson get settled in the living room .and I'll be right in to help."

"You don't have to help me, honey," Mrs. Albertson said, holding onto the table as she stepped toward the living room. "I have lived alone in this house for over two decades. I believe I can find my recliner and pull the lever without a lick of trouble."

"But." Callie's eyes scanned the dining room. "Where's your walker?"

"It's waiting by the front door, I think," Mrs. Albertson said, walking past Callie. "Or either in the kitchen or the hallway by the bathroom. Sometimes I forget where I put it when I'm inside."

Callie hovered behind Mrs. Albertson until she was sitting down in her recliner. The walker wasn't in the living room either. Mrs. Albertson adjusted an orange crocheted afghan across her legs before Callie turned and headed toward the kitchen. She stopped and picked up the tea pitcher and the almost empty gravy boat from the dining room table. This truly had been the best meal she had eaten in ages. Fiona could cook, but not like this. Her lips pushed up into a distant smile as she imagined the look on her family's face if she brought something this good to Thanksgiving at the end of the week. Of course, she usually didn't bring anything, but this year was different. She had a steady job and could afford to help with the meal, even if it was to just to buy the brown and serve rolls and a pie to pop in the oven.

Callie stepped into the kitchen and stopped. Honor stood near the sink, rolling up the sleeves of his white dress shirt. Callie's eyes took in his muscular forearms as his hands quickly flipped the white fabric up to his elbows. Her mouth went dry as she imagined those arms wrapping around her, pulling her close.

"Here." Honor looked up, and Callie blinked, feeling the heat rise in her cheeks. "Hand me those," he said, reaching out and taking the dishes from her hands.

His fingers brushed against hers, and she swallowed, trying to get some moisture to return to her mouth. "I'm glad we're talking again," she said, the words coming out breathlessly, as her body reacted to the innocent touch. "I've been worried about you all week long."

Honor took the dishes from her hands and sat them on the counter behind him. "I heard something that upset me." He kept his back toward her as he turned on the water at the sink. "I didn't handle the news very well. I'm sorry about that. I shouldn't have brought my problems to work with me."

"You're only human, Duck." Callie stepped up next to him and picked up the dish soap, squirting a stream into his side of the sink. "As long as you're okay, and." She paused and set the bottle back on the narrow counter ledge behind the sink. "And as long as we're okay, that's all that matters." Her arm pressed against his as he turned the faucet to her sink. The heat of his touch, his arm pressed snugly against hers, caused her heart to do a funny little flip. She looked out the kitchen window in front of them to Mrs. Albertson's back yard. A skinny orange cat with a big head and a crook in the end of his tail lay stretched in the orange and brown leaves scattered across the lawn. Callie swallowed, but she still didn't have any wetness in her mouth. *Get yourself together, girl. You can't react like this every time he gets close. He might not feel like you do. You can't throw yourself at him like you did Dawson. He's your boss—and your friend. And you're not that person anymore.*

"Callie."

Honor's deep voice was so close she felt his breath on her cheek. Callie turned and looked into his green eyes, inches away from hers. "Yeah?" The word came out as a whisper. Her heart pounded with his nearness, and he turned. Even closer.

"I need to talk to you about something." Honor's hand reached up, white soap suds dancing on his fingers as he pushed a strand of Callie's blond hair away from her cheek. "It's important."

Callie looked down from his eyes, deep and intense, staring at her, the look causing her to burn inside, to his lips as they whispered whatever it was he was saying. She tilted her chin up as his face came closer, his lips landing on hers. Her arms stretched up and found their way around his neck as he reached around her, pulling her closer, lifting her up off the ground. The heat that had started in her face earlier was now everywhere inside of her, drawing her closer to Honor. The touch of his lips against hers, his chest pulled close against her, made her forget everything else, where she was, what she was doing. All she wanted was to stay right where she was, in the moment.

Honor's lips left Callie's and trailed over to her ear. "We need to talk," he whispered, his voice husky. He pressed his lips against the lobe of her ear for a brief moment, and Callie pulled in a breath of hot air, blowing it out against his neck. "We need to talk," he said again, his voice choking out the words.

A new sensation started above Callie's waist. Something wet, cool—and very wet. Honor pulled away and Callie blinked, her body trying to acclimate to the absence of his touch. She looked at his face, his eyes wide with surprise.

"We are making a mess." The corners of his lips turned up into a grin as he looked away from her and to the over-flowing sink. He let go of her arms and turned, cutting off the water.

Callie watched as he turned off the faucet, her mind finally coming back from where he had taken her a few seconds before. She looked down at her dress, an enormous dripping wet spot covering her front. She stared down at the puddle of water at their feet. "I made it through the entire meal without spilling a drop of food on me," she said, her eyes twinkling with laughter. She looked over at Honor's wet trousers at his belt line. "At least I'm not alone."

Honor reached into one sink and then the other, letting some of the water out. "Go see if Mrs. Albertson has some-thing dry you can put on. I'll get this done."

"You sure?" Callie's dress was much wetter than Honor's pants, since she was nearest to the sink that had actually run over. "I hate to leave you to do the work."

"I can have this done by the time you find something dry to put on. Believe me, the banana pudding is worth whatever I have to do in here." He lifted his arm from the sink and grabbed a dish towel, mopping up the water along the edge of the sink. "And Callie, we *really* need to talk."

"Yeah. I agree."

Callie grabbed another dishtowel from a basket on the counter by the stove and sopped the water from her dress as she walked back to the living room. What had happened in there? Had she done anything to initiate that kiss? No, not intentionally, anyway. It just sort of... happened, but wow. Even thinking about their kiss made her cheeks warm.

"What happened to you, honey?"

Callie stopped in the living room doorway and pulled her lips into a friendly smile, away from whatever look had been on her face while she daydreamed about the kiss. "I wasn't paying attention and let my sink overflow." She lifted the towel from the front of her dress. "Luckily, my dress caught most of the water, and didn't flood your kitchen. Honor's mopping up the counter and the floor."

"You soaked your whole dress to the bone." Mrs. Albertson's eyes danced with laughter. "Y'all must have been having an awful lot of fun cleaning my ole kitchen if you didn't see the sink running over."

Callie tilted her head down and raised an eyebrow. *The old fox. She sent us in there together on purpose. Well, let her play matchmaker. It obviously worked.* "We were in a rush so we could get to your banana pudding." No need to give her any of the details. She still wasn't sure exactly what had happened herself. "You don't happen to have a pair of sweatpants and a t-shirt or anything I could put on so I won't have to go home and change, do you?"

"I'm afraid my jogging pants would fall to your ankles. We're close to the same height, but that's where the similarity stops." Mrs. Albertson's eyes narrowed, and she looked toward the back of the house. "I have a clean muu-muu hanging on the back of my bathroom door, though. It is an extra-large, but it's dry and will keep you covered while that pretty dress dries. Will that do?"

"It will do perfectly." Callie stepped back into the dining room and through another doorway that led into a tiny hallway. She smiled and shook her head. The walker stood next to an open door leading into a compact little bathroom. The stumpy little hallway, really more of an alcove, had a doorway on either end, each open with a bedroom on the other side.

Callie stepped across the hallway and into the bathroom, shutting the door behind her. The sound of dishes bumping together floated from the kitchen. She unbuttoned the front of her corduroy dress and peeled it away from the soaked slip underneath. She slipped the straps of the slip off of her shoulders and stepped out. She draped both garments over the shower rod behind her and dried the rest of the dampness off with the kitchen towel. She looked around the bathroom. The old bathtub, not a fancy clawfoot tub, but an old metal one, took up the wall behind her. A little window with opaque glass let in faint sunlight from the far side of the tub. The sink, square with no counter around it, held a denture cup on one side and a round, peach colored canister of powder on the other side. A medicine cabinet with a mirror for the door hung above it. The toilet set across from the bathtub between the outlet door and another very narrow door, probably leading to a closet. A bottle of perfume with a label Callie didn't recognize set next to a roll of toilet paper. She picked up the bottle, took off the top, and sniffed. A soft floral scent tickled her nose, a scent perfect for Mrs. Albertson. She put the top back on the perfume and took the cotton muu-muu from the hook on the back of the bathroom door. She smiled at her reflection in the full-length mirror on the door. The enormous pink and yellow house dress hung on her like a tent, but she was dry and could eat as much banana pudding as she wanted in this thing. She snapped the last snap and slipped off her high-heeled pumps. They looked kind of ridiculous in her current attire.

CHAPTER TWENTY

*C*allie closed her eyes and let out a moan as the banana pudding rolled across her tongue. "Oh. My. Word. This is the best ever."

"Told ya," Honor said, smiling, as he stuck his spoon back in the bowl for another bite. "Mrs. Albertson, you could sell this stuff and make a killing."

"No, banana pudding's not for selling, it's for sharing with the people you care about." Mrs. Albertson lifted her spoon to her lips. "It's not hard to make, anyway. I can teach you both."

"Can you, really?" Callie's eyes stretched wide as she stared across the living room at Mrs. Albertson, her legs raised up in her recliner, the bowl of pudding on her lap. "If I brought a bowl of this stuff to Thanksgiving and told my family that I actually made it, I would be." She paused and licked the back of her spoon. "Well, I don't know what I would be, but believe me, everybody there would think I was lying. I would have to call you and get you to back me up," she said, looking over at Honor. "It would be so great."

"Well, why don't I give you a little grocery list, and you

come by Wednesday afternoon?" Mrs. Albertson winked at Callie. "I'll give you your very first lesson on how to make banana pudding."

"Wednesday." Callie licked a dab of pudding off her lower lip and turned to look at Honor sitting on the couch beside her. "How late are we working Wednesday? We have that presentation Tuesday evening, but nothing else for the rest of the week, if I'm remembering correctly."

"That's right." Honor nodded. "We'll set up the new account Wednesday morning if the school system you're meeting with on Tuesday decides to use our software. That way, it will be ready to go when they come back from Thanksgiving break on Monday. You can do your usual follow up call with whoever your contact is from the school board while Clutch and I do the tech stuff. Other than that, it should be a slow day. I'm not going to schedule anything for the rest of the week. School will be out, and nobody wants to talk school software over a holiday break."

"Alright then," Callie said, turning back to Mrs. Albertson. "It's a deal. Will three o'clock Wednesday work for you?"

"Sounds good to me. You can make a big bowl for your family, and I'll make a big bowl for mine." Mrs. Albertson looked at Honor. "You might as well come over too and make a big bowl for your family as well, son. We can have our own little pudding party."

"I guess I'll pass." Honor raked his spoon across the bottom of his dessert bowl, getting the last bit on his spoon. "My father is having Thanksgiving with his new wife in Houston, so I will be flying solo on Thursday."

Callie pulled her spoon through her puckered lips and pointed it at Honor. "No, we can't let you do that. Nobody should spend Thanksgiving alone. You can go to Fiona's with me."

"That's not necessary," Honor said, his eyes softening at

Callie's invitation. "I don't want to intrude on your family time."

"Are you kidding?" Callie dipped her spoon back in her bowl and brought out another bite. "They are always ragging me about not having a boyfriend. We can do like they do in those Hallmark movies that come on over the holidays. You can be my fake boyfriend for Thanksgiving. Except, of course, we won't tell them that. We'll be straight with them and tell them you're my poor lonely boss who I am helping out by giving a free meal."

"Of course," Honor said, reaching over and wiping a spot of yellow pudding from the corner of Callie's mouth. "We wouldn't want to give them the wrong idea."

"Oh." Callie's eyes followed Honor's finger as it moved away from the corner of her mouth and rested on his lips. He licked off the pudding, and she swallowed. "We won't have to *give* them any ideas," she said, pushing down the boulder in her throat. "They will come up with them all on their own." *Why does his touch make me so squishy inside?*

"Callie, honey." Mrs. Albertson watched the young couple from across the room, a pleased expression settling on her face. "I noticed you whispered something in Malcom's ear while we were leaving church. As a matter of fact, you whispered something in the preacher's ear, too."

"Yes, ma'am." Callie set the empty dessert bowl on the coffee table next to Honor's and picked up her cup of coffee. "I meant to tell both of you at lunch about that, but I got too caught up with eating. You have been so nice to me today," she said, smiling at Mrs. Albertson. "And Honor," she cut her eyes to the side, "is practically my best friend, so I wanted to tell both of you."

"Have at it, honey. I'm dying to know what you said that made both of those men smile so big."

"Me too," Honor said, his voice much more subdued.

"Yesterday, after talking with my sister about... something." Callie sniffed and reached down and straightened the muu-muu where her knee was poking through the gap between two of the snaps running down the front. "I still get emotional thinking about it." She looked, first at Mrs. Albertson, then Honor, her eyes wet with unshed tears. "Yesterday, I gave my life to Jesus. I know both of you probably did that a long time ago, but it's all new to me. I am so overwhelmed with this feeling of gratitude that I just have to tell people, especially people who have talked to me about Jesus before. Malcolm used to always tell me he was praying for me when he would come see Nana back when she was still living at home and getting home health. He was Nana's nurse and he's a really nice guy."

"That's what you were doing?" Honor's eyebrows raised, and he stared at Callie. He slumped back against the couch and looked away toward the window across the room.

"Yes." Callie said, the words slowly trailing off as she stared at Honor. "I knew they would be happy for me. Why? What's wrong?"

"Nothing." Honor ran his hand over his jawline as a slow smile crept across his face. His eyes turned back to Callie's questioning gaze. "You made a profession of faith? Yesterday?"

"Yes, Honor." Callie slowly nodded her head like she was talking to a two-year-old. "That's what I just said."

"Well." Honor clapped his hands together and sat back up. "That's just wonderful," he said, his voice suddenly full of energy. "I mean." He reached over and straightened his coffee mug on its coaster. "That is great, and I'm so happy for you. Congratulations."

*T*he kiss. Honor lay back in his bed and let what happened in Mrs. Albertson's kitchen play over in his mind. He was a one-woman guy. He had known that about himself for a long time. He didn't date much, only a few times in college, and none in high school. The girls he had taken out were usually women Clutch had introduced him to, and he never went on a second date with any of them.

Going through college and starting his business had always been at the forefront of his mind. When he became financially secure, he would decide where he wanted to live, find a girl, get married, and start a family. He had always had a plan.

He thought the plan was going along in the right direction when he started dating Sheila. He figured they would date for two or three years, then settle into a routine. He would buy a house in the suburbs of Houston, and then they would marry. Then he got blindsided. When she left him high and dry for the jock-friend of hers, he had thrown the marriage part of his plan out the window, or at least put it on hold for a while.

After Sheila was gone, and his dad remarried, Honor decided it was time to expand his business and his life. That's when he moved back to Carson's Bayou. Forget the marriage part. He would buy a house and put down roots. If a woman came along eventually that wanted the same things he wanted, fine. If she didn't, at least he would be living in the town where he grew up, where he had a few friends.

But today—that kiss. Sheila's kisses had never affected him like that. Making him want to keep…. He flipped over and punched up his pillow, not allowing his mind to go where it was headed. He had known he loved Callie before, but now there was no doubt. If he was honest with himself, he not only loved her, he wanted her too. That wasn't a bad thing, really. Well, not if she felt the same about him and wanted the same things in her life that he wanted in his, like stability, and eventually, kids.

He would ask Callie out. Not on a work thing, but on a real date. Her past didn't matter. She had aborted the baby when she didn't know the Lord. Now. Now that she was a Christian, they could talk about how God made every life as a precious gift. Talk about how each child had the right to live, no matter what the circumstances. If she hadn't felt the same way before, she would study the Scripture and come around.

Honor stared through the darkness to the moonlight filtering in through the curtain on the other side of the room. Was he wanting her to come around in her thinking because she needed to grow in Christ, or because he wanted to date a woman with the same values as him? Was it because he wanted to eventually marry a woman who valued family, wanted to be the mother of his children?

Clutch was right. He had to talk to her about what Dawson Wallace had told him. He should have done it earlier today, but after they finished eating their dessert, she said she had to go. She was babysitting for her brother that after-noon. He flopped onto his back. It was going to be okay, though. He had time to get things straight. They were talking again, and he would find the opportunity to get alone with her and discuss this. It would all work out. Callie wasn't going anywhere. Even if it took a couple of years. They could start dating and move slow. Make plans for their future together. His tongue darted out and ran across his lower lip. Not too slow, though. The feeling of her lips against his pushed to the front of his mind. No, they couldn't move too slow.

He would go to Thanksgiving dinner with her on Thursday, then talk with her that evening when he brought her home. In the meantime, they would continue as friends. He would have to reign in this attraction that was growing so fast that it was as out of control as kudzu weeds. Clutch could go with them Tuesday to do the presentation. It wouldn't take all three of them, but he didn't trust himself to be shut up alone in a car with Callie for the hour drive to the school and the hour drive back. Plus, there was the dinner they would share after they were done with the meeting. He could just let her and Clutch go. No. He wanted to go with her, spend time with her. Clutch would wonder why they were all three going, or maybe he wouldn't. Clutch was pretty smart.

After Thanksgiving, after their talk, they would move forward. Callie had to have feelings for him. She would not have responded to his kiss the way she had if she only thought of him as a friend. Friends didn't kiss each other. Not like that.

CHAPTER TWENTY-ONE

*M*onday morning, Clutch rested his hip on the corner of Honor's desk. "I take it you talked to Callie." He had walked in to work about twenty minutes before and found Callie and Honor acting like old friends again. "Did you two get everything worked out?"

"No, not yet." Honor looked past Clutch toward the hallway. "Where did she go anyway?"

"She wanted a pumpkin spice whatever coffee from the Bayou Bean. Said she would be back in a few minutes." Clutch reached down and straightened a manila folder on Honor's desk. "Well, something has changed since Friday. Both of you are acting like a couple of lovebirds again, maybe even worse than before."

"Did she tell you she became a Christian over the weekend?" Honor hit a stroke on his keyboard, then leaned back in his chair, and looked at Clutch. "She told me yesterday after church at Mrs. Albertson's house."

"Yeah, she told me. We plan on getting together to do a little Bible study a couple of times a week during lunch." Clutch fiddled with an ink pen in a cup by his leg. "So, you two are honkey-dory now? All on the same page? Come on man, give me some details. You looked like death warmed over Friday. I didn't talk to you Saturday or Sunday, and today you are walking around on cloud nine. Spill it. There's more going on here than you are letting on."

"I can't." Honor cradled both hands behind his head and leaned back in his chair. "At least not until she and I talk this thing out, the thing I was worried about last week."

"Okay." Clutch's brow furrowed as he stared down at his best friend. "You still haven't talked to her and worked things out, but you two are chummy again—and the only thing that's changed is she became a Christian." He raised an eyebrow and continued to watch Honor for a couple of seconds as he thought everything through. "I think I've got it now."

"Got it?" Honor pulled his shoulders back and felt them pop in a couple of places. He did not sleep well at all last night. "What did you get?"

"You decided that if God could forgive her for whatever she had done that had you so upset, that you could forgive her too."

Honor dropped his hands to his side and frowned. "I hadn't really thought about it that way." He looked at Clutch, but his mind's eye saw Callie, smiling at him yesterday with damp eyes as she told him about her decision to follow Christ. "You know what? You're right. You're exactly right." Honor blinked. "I'm being an idiot."

"It's not the first time, my friend."

"Yeah, yeah." Honor waved his hand in Clutch's direction. "It won't be the last either. I know."

"Since you two are back to your normal selves, do you need me to go with Callie tomorrow night to the presentation, or are you taking back over?"

"We are all three going." Honor watched Clutch's brow

pull down again. He sat up and looked at the computer screen, avoiding his gaze. "Don't ask any questions. I have my reasons."

"I'm sure you do." Clutch pushed up from the corner of the desk. "You're the boss, boss. I'm just the VP of the company. No need to tell me anything."

Callie pulled her sweater around her shoulders and trotted across the street to her Volkswagen. She had only seen Dawson skulking around a couple of times last week, but he was back at it this morning. It was still early, eight thirty, but he had already pulled his Mustang in behind her car.

Dawson rolled down the passenger's window as Callie drew near. "I see you're still working there. I figured he would have cut you loose already."

"I'm still here, and I'm going to be here, so you need to stop whatever this is you are doing and go on about your business." Callie leaned down and looked in the car window. "Aren't you supposed to be leaving for school? What about this scholarship you said you got?"

"I start next semester, after the first of the year. It's some kind of special deal my dad worked out with the coach." Dawson leaned across the car console and smiled up at Callie like he used to when they were dating. "Where are you headed? You just got to work."

"To the Bayou Bean." Callie glanced over her shoulder toward her office. The coffee run had been an excuse to come across the street and put an end to this. She had to get rid of Dawson. Honor wouldn't fire her because of a crazy ex-boyfriend, but he would confront him. That became apparent the last time the three of them were together. "Look. I don't know what you want from me. We broke up, you started dating other people. Why are you doing this now? You know we are over."

"Lindsey broke up with me." Dawson grabbed the door handle and the car door opened a crack. "She didn't hold a candle to you anyway, Callie. Just get in and let me drive you to get your coffee. If you will let me talk to you, I promise I will leave you alone if that's what you really want."

Callie pulled the door open and bent down where she could see him better. "Do you mean it? This will be the last time I find you in front of my office?"

"If you will hear me out, and I can't change your mind, I will leave you alone. I'm leaving after Christmas, anyway. I just need to see you, you know, like old times, one more time."

I shouldn't do this. Callie slid onto the cool black leather seat and shut the door. "This is definitely not like old times, so don't get any ideas. You are going to take me to get my coffee. We will talk, and you will drive me back. Then we are done." She pulled her seatbelt across her chest. "Got it?"

"Sure. We'll get your coffee and drive while we talk. I talk better with something in my hands." Dawson pulled into the street and headed down the short distance to the coffee shop. "If it can't be you." He flashed a knowing grin at Callie. "It will have to be the steering wheel of my car. Here." He pulled into a parking spot and took a fifty out of his console. "Get whatever you want. It's on me."

"No, thanks." Callie rolled her eyes and unbuckled her seat belt. "I can buy my own coffee. Like I have been trying to tell you, things are not like they used to be." *What did I ever see in this guy?*

Callie got out and slammed the car door. She hurried into

the coffee shop and the familiar smell of fresh pastries and rich, newly roasted coffee tempted her senses. She stepped into the line behind a couple of older ladies and slipped her phone from the pocket of her sweater. *Ran into someone. Will be back soon. Explain when I see you.*

She pushed send and eased up to the counter as the ladies moved away with warm glazed donuts and steaming hot drinks. Her phone vibrated as she placed her order. She looked down at the text from Honor when the barista turned to get her coffee. *Take your time. Be safe. See you when you get back.* Her lips turned up in a smile as she slipped the phone back into her sweater pocket. Would he ask her out today? If he hadn't asked her out by Thanksgiving, she would take the bull by the horns and ask him out. It was time to move beyond friends.

Callie paid for her coffee and looked around the shop, smiling at a couple of people she had seen at the church yesterday. An unexpected wave of nostalgia washed over her. Did she really want to leave Carson's Bayou? The shadow of a frown settled on her face as she started toward the door. She had been so sure she wanted to move away before she started this job, before Honor reentered her life, before she had given her life to Christ. She would be leaving all of her family and, and what? She used to think that was all she had holding her to the small town, but now she was not so sure.

"Okay." Callie sat in the car seat and shut the door. She reached back for the seat belt, but it hung up, refusing to pull over her chest. She tugged again, almost spilling the Styrofoam coffee cup in her hands. "I can't be gone but for a few minutes, so let's talk." She let go of the seat belt and looked at Dawson's red-rimmed eyes. "Why have you been following me?"

"Remember how we used to come here before history class and get bear claws and coffee? Half the football team would be here with us." Dawson whipped into the street and punched the gas pedal, ignoring her question. "Those were fun days."

Callie brought her cup up with the motion of the car, careful not to spill the coffee. "Yes, I remember." She raised the large dark roast blend, heavily flavored with pumpkin-spice creamer to her lips. "I also remember that you laced your coffee with milk and vodka." She took a sip and lowered the cup. It was still too hot to drink. "As a matter of fact, you laced almost everything with vodka."

"You didn't complain." Dawson continued through town, businesses flying by the window in a blur. "We used to be happy, had a lot of fun. I always figured, you know, after the baby thing was over, that you'd come back to me."

"The baby thing?" Callie turned her hips in the car seat and glared at Dawson, her lips pushed together in a firm line, her eyes shooting darts in his direction. "I was pregnant, Dawson. Pregnant with our child. If I had not miscarried, we would be parents of a four-month-old right now."

"I know." Dawson glanced at Callie, then turned his eyes back to the road ahead. "But you miscarried, right? I've been watching you, waiting. I gave you time to get over all of that, but it's been long enough. It's time for us to get over all that and get back together."

"Are you kidding me?" Callie's voice climbed higher, along with her temper. She grabbed the dash as Dawson punched the gas and flew around the car in front of them. They had made it out of Carson's Bayou and were now on a narrow country road. "I told you when I broke up with you that we were done, that I would raise the baby on my own."

"But there's no baby, Callie. I've given you plenty of time to get over that." Dawson tightened his knuckles on the steering wheel as he pressed down on the gas pedal. "This isn't about me and our kid. You aren't fooling me. This is about that boss of yours. You think he's got the hots for you. You think that if you throw yourself at him like you did me, he's going to set you up nice and cushy." Dawson laughed, the sound hard and bitter. "You've seen what he drives, how he dresses. Even if he has money stuck away somewhere, he won't be spending it on you. I thought you were smarter than that."

"Shut up." Callie pulled in a deep breath and looked out her passenger's window at the blur of cow fields flying by. This was a mistake. She never should have agreed to get in the car with him. "You don't know what you're talking about," she said, turning to look at Dawson. "Honor is a good, honest guy, but he is not the reason that I won't give you another chance. I am not who I was, and I will never go back to being that person again. Now, take me…"

The rest of the sentence faded from Callie's lips as she felt herself flying forward, her arm slamming into the dash, spilling the hot coffee all over her chest. A truck pulling a trailer of enormous round hay bales coming over the hill toward them flashed into her line of vision. Dawson raced around the tractor ahead of him and into the truck's lane. She didn't have time to think as the Mustang left the road, dodging the oncoming truck and trailer. The car was airborne for a few seconds, and so was Callie, sailing up and forward. When the Mustang connected with the massive trunk of the ancient oak tree, Callie's head connected with the windshield, the smell of pumpkin spice coffee filling her nose as the blackness overtook her.

CHAPTER TWENTY-TWO

*H*onor jingled the change in his pocket as he stared out the large window of the office lobby. "Her car's still there. She never walks anywhere."

"Text her or call her and check on her if you're that worried." Clutch looked over from his nearby desk. "It's only been a little over an hour, but if you're really worried, check in with her."

Honor pulled out his phone and unlocked the screen. *Hey, just check.* He erased the text and slipped it back in his pocket. "No. She said she bumped into somebody, and I told her not to hurry. She probably is talking with them and hasn't looked at the time."

"You could always walk down to the coffee shop and see."

"No. That would be acting too much like that ex-boyfriend of hers." He jingled the change again, then reached over, and rubbed the leaf of the peace lily she had picked out to put in the window back when she first started. That seemed like such a long time ago. "I'll give her thirty more minutes and then text."

"I can talk to that guy if you need me to. I almost did this morning, but I decided to ask you about it first." Clutch leaned back in his chair and swiveled it toward the window. Honor continued to stare across the street, like a guard dog waiting for his master to return. "I can approach him from a business side. Tell him he's taking a parking space for a potential customer, or something like that—not from an emotional place, like I imagine you would."

"I'm afraid I would end up coming to blows with the guy if I tried to talk to him," Honor said, turning from the window. "From what I can tell, the man is a childish jerk who stays drunk about half the time."

Honor walked away from the window and across the room to his office door. Clutch rolled his chair back closer to his desk, but stopped when Honor spun on his heels and marched back to the window again. "Did you say his Mustang was out there this morning? I got here before seven, and the street was clear."

"Yeah." Clutch stood and stepped over to the window beside his friend. "He pulled in right behind Callie's car as I was walking across the street. I talked to her about him before she left for coffee. I told her that tomorrow she could park in my spot behind the building, and I would park over there."

"I thought he was leaving her alone." Honor rubbed his hand across his jawline. I didn't see him there last week.

"He was there a couple of mornings, but he left before noon." Clutch smiled and nodded to an old man and woman walking down the sidewalk together in front of their office. A gust of wind caused a crunchy brown leaf to swirl around their legs as they hurried along. Honor ignored the couple and continued to stare at Callie's Volkswagen.

"She said she would not change her parking spot and give the guy the satisfaction of thinking he was bothering her," Clutch said, turning to look at his friend. "I told her if she changed her mind to let me know. Do you think something's wrong?"

"I'm not sure." Honor's brow pulled low. "I should have handled this before now, though. That guy is nothing but trouble."

The office phone rang, and Clutch stepped over to his desk and answered it. Honor pulled his cell phone from his pocket again. No messages. Undoubtably, she would not have gone anywhere with that guy. If Honor hadn't already seen how the man tried to intimidate Callie, he wouldn't be worried about her. Callie stood up to her ex the night of the party, and from the way Clutch talked, she was not the least bit scared of him. That was part of the reason he was worried. She had a tendency to act first and think later.

"That was Langston Wade." Clutch set the phone back in its cradle. "We need to get to the hospital."

Honor stared at Clutch, ice wrapping around his heart. "Is she okay? What did he do to her?"

"She's been in an accident." Clutch grabbed his jacket from the back of his chair. "I'll drive. Come on." He flipped the light switches by the door and held it open as Honor followed him out. "Wade said he would fill you in when you get there. He called you since you're her boss."

Honor mechanically followed Clutch out of the building and to his truck, listening to what he was saying as thoughts bombarded his brain. He had been sitting on his high horse, judging Callie, his friend, and the woman he loved. He had not offered to help her deal with what she was going through. He had not even been willing to talk to her about it because he thought he was so much better than her.

Hadn't his own passion lit up with their one simple kiss yesterday? It had affected him so deeply that it scared him to be alone with her. He might touch her again and lose control. What gave him the right to abandon her because she had made a mistake and then taken the easy road out? He was sure that Dawson Wallace had not supported her when he found out about the baby. He had not supported her when he found out about it, either. He was so concerned about trusting her, but the truth was—could she trust him?

Honor stared out the truck window, not seeing the scenery moving past as Clutch drove them to the hospital. Abortion was a terrible thing, but did he have the right to act the way he did when he found out about it? No. He sat, unmoving, staring straight ahead as they pulled into the parking lot near the front of the hospital. He should have reached out to her, been a friend, a Christian friend who loved her in spite of her past, the way God had loved her. The way God had loved and forgiven him. *Lord, forgive me my arrogance and pride. It has truly blinded me. Help me make this right with her. Don't let me be too late.*

"You alright, man?"

Honor blinked and looked over at Clutch staring at him. "Yeah." He rubbed his eyes and looked out toward the hospital. An ambulance was pulling in with its lights flashing over near the emergency room entrance. "Did Wade say how bad it was?"

"She's pretty banged up." Clutch's eyes softened with compassion. He opened his truck door and repeated what he had already told Honor a few minutes before during the drive over. "Langston said she was unconscious, and they had just gotten her in to do the x-rays. Come on. Let's go check on her."

Honor nodded, his lips pushed together in a thin line. He had to focus on the here and now. Wallowing in self-pity would not help Callie. He got out of the truck and walked across the parking lot with Clutch to the waiting area of the hospital.

Langston Wade, in his expensive black suit, almost as tall

as Clutch, would have been easy to pick out of the different people sitting and standing around the large ice-cold lobby, even if Honor didn't know what the man looked like. Honor looked across the room, away from the sliding glass doors at the entrance to a set of chairs where Langston Wade stood, talking with Sydney Madison, Callie's brother. The two looked odd grouped together, Sydney in coveralls with grease stains, and Langston looking like he had stepped out of a magazine. Honor and Clutch hurried over. Honor noticed Fiona Wade sitting with another woman he didn't recognize, probably Callie's sister-in-law. That was all the family she had.

Honor shook hands with the men and spoke to the ladies. His eyes darted to the double doors that led to the working part of the hospital where Callie was, where he wanted to be. He listened, forcing himself to concentrate, as Fiona told them what she knew.

"She was driving Dawson Wallace's car out on Sawmill road. She tried to pass a tractor and almost ran into an oncoming truck." Tears filled Fiona's eyes, and she dabbed them with a tissue. "She swerved and went off the road and hit a tree. The police said she must have been going close to one hundred miles an hour."

"Was she alone?" Honor's eyes narrowed as he listened to what she was saying. Why was she driving his car? Why was she even in his car?

"No." Langston Wade sat down beside Fiona and wrapped his arm around her, pulling her close. "No, the trooper that I talked to said Dawson Wallace was with her. He said there were a lot of empty alcohol bottles on the backseat floorboard. Do you think Callie was taking the man somewhere because he was too drunk to drive?"

"It's possible," Clutch said when Honor didn't answer. He stuck his hand out and shook Langston's. He offered his hand to Sidney and the rest of the group. "High. I'm Clutch Franklin. I work with Callie and Honor. I spoke with you on the phone a while ago."

Honor listened as everyone around them chatted in low tones, trying to figure out what happened. Sydney Madison didn't say much, just nodded every once in a while, but Honor remembered the man as always being quiet. Honor answered questions directed at him, but mostly stared at the double doors over near the gift shop, praying someone would walk through with some good news. He couldn't tell them anything Clutch hadn't already said anyway. Clutch had been a better friend to Callie over the last week than he had. If he had done what he should, talked to Callie and helped her deal with Dawson Wallace, she wouldn't be back there lying on a gurney unconscious, possibly fighting for her life.

He looked down at the little cup of coffee somebody had put in his hands, sending up more prayers for Callie. If she would be okay, he would be to her whatever she wanted. Friend, boss, whatever she wanted. He needed to tell her how he felt, how wrong he was for pushing her away. Whatever she did with that, he would accept.

An hour crept by as Honor sat silently, staring at the double doors. Finally, a squatty man in wrinkled green scrubs stepped through the doors and walked over to where they all sat. Honor stood and listened as Fiona asked about her sister.

"She has a nasty concussion, several fractured ribs, a broken collarbone, and the radial bone of her right arm is broken. She's bruised up from one end to the other." The doctor rubbed his hands together and looked around at the faces staring at him. "From what I understand about the accident, she should have looked a lot worse. She's one lucky lady."

"You're saying she's going to be okay?" Fiona asked.

"She's still unconscious. We won't know for sure what's going on with her brain until she wakes up. She had a severe blow to the head. Once the swelling goes down in her brain, we are hopeful that she will be fine, pending no complications."

"Can we see her?" Honor asked, speaking for the first time in over an hour.

"She's in ICU." The doctor turned to Honor. "Once they get her cleaned up and set up in the room, they will let you go in. Are you family?"

"Uh, no. Her friend."

"Oh, well, she's going to need all of you when she wakes up. She's young and healthy, but she is still going to need a lot of help to get back on her feet."

"Don't worry, doctor," Langston Wade said, a confident tone in his voice. "We will be there for her and make sure she has everything she needs. You let me know what she needs, and I will make it happen."

Honor moved upstairs to the ICU waiting room, along with Callie's family. Clutch said he was going to run an errand and would be back later. Another hour crept by. The nurse finally allowed visitors to come in two at a time. Fiona and Sidney went in first. When they stepped back out several minutes later, Fiona was pale, and Sidney's eyes were wet.

"She can have one more couple, then she will need to rest again," the nurse said, looking at their group.

"You go ahead," Langston said, patting Honor on the shoulder. "I will see her next time."

Honor looked at Langston and nodded his head, unable to speak again. The woman, the sister-in-law, had stepped over to the far window where she was whispering with Sidney. He swallowed the knot in his throat and stepped toward the door. "Thank you," he finally choked out.

Honor followed the nurse through the doors. The temperature dropped ten degrees. The nurse's shoes were silent on the shiny linoleum floor. Everything was silent except the tap of Honor's shoes as they stepped up to the glass wall. Callie lay on the other side.

The nurse opened the see-through door, and he followed her in, his breath catching in his throat. Callie's forehead bulged out. Both eyes were swollen closed and horrible shades of purple and black. The swelling extended down her face, misshaping her nose and lips. A brace was around her neck, and her head was wrapped in bandages. Her body was hidden under the blankets, but her left arm was on top of the covers with an IV connected to her forearm. Monitors silently flashed readings behind the bed. Bags of IV fluids hung from poles on the other side of the bed. Tears filled Honor's eyes, blurring his vision as he stepped up next to the bed beside the nurse. How had he let this happen?

"Talk to her." The nurse said softly. "She made a noise a while ago, so she can probably hear you. She needs to know she's not alone."

"Callie." Honor reached down to touch her, then pulled his hand back, not wanting to cause her any more pain. "It's Duck, Oatmeal." Honor cleared his throat and leaned in closer, whispering in her ear. "I'm so sorry, Callie. I love you." He looked at her face, praying for any sign that she heard him, but she lay there. Not moving.

CHAPTER TWENTY-THREE

*H*onor walked out of the ICU room and found Clutch waiting for him. He wouldn't be able to go in to visit Callie again for at least two hours, maybe longer, if the rest of the family used up that block of time with her. There was no need to sit there and let his thoughts wear him down. But what could he do? Going back to work was out of the question. That would be useless. Clutch suggested they go grab some food. It was after noon and neither of them had eaten. When they stepped into the elevator, Clutch told him where he had been.

"I went to Dawson Wallace's room and talked to him." Clutch pushed the elevator button and looked at Honor. "I know he was just in a terrible wreck, but he seemed very defensive to me."

"He's here?" Honor jerked his head up from where he had been staring at the floor tiles, tan with a swirl of dark brown mixed in. "What did he say?"

"He said Callie came over to his car, and he offered to take her to get a coffee. He said when they came out of the coffee shop, she wanted to drive his car, like old times. That guy is a real piece of work. He swears that he begged Callie to slow down, but she was laughing and having a good time, and the car got away from her.

"I don't believe him."

"Well, neither do I," Clutch said, frowning at his friend. "The way she talked about him this morning, there's no way she would go joy riding with the guy. He's lying to cover something up. I bet you money he's been drinking."

"I wish there was someone to talk to who could find that out." Honor waited as the elevator doors slid open, then stepped into the lobby. "The doctors and nurses can't tell us anything about his personal records." His eyes traveled around the large room to the different groups of people standing and sitting, waiting for information about a friend or loved one, or waiting to go up and visit them. He looked at the information desk on the far side of the lobby, then on over to the little coffee bar manned by a couple of pink ladies. A cop leaned against the counter, chatting with one of the women as she pulled out a cookie from behind the little counter and placed it in a piece of waxed paper. "You don't happen to know any of the police in this town, do you?"

"A deputy goes to our church. He's that red-headed man that sits near the front every Sunday." Clutch looked over to where the cop was paying for his coffee and snack. "Why don't we try asking that guy if he knows anything about the wreck? It can't hurt to try."

Honor walked with Clutch across the lobby where the policeman was standing. They introduced themselves and told how they knew Callie. The man was polite and seemed genuinely concerned about how she was doing.

"She's still unconscious," Honor said, a picture of her swollen face flashing across his eyes. "I doubt you will be able to talk to her for a while."

"I figured as much." The policeman stepped away from

the coffee counter as a couple of women walked up to place their order. Honor and Clutch followed him over to an area where no one could hear them talking. "We've already looked at her blood alcohol level. She hadn't been drinking."

"We can vouch for that," Clutch said. "What about that guy? The one she was with."

"His blood alcohol level was over the legal limit to be driving. Which isn't surprising. The back floorboard of the car is full of vodka bottles and beer bottles." The officer popped the black lid off of his coffee cup and took a sip of the hot drink. "The guy says that your friend wanted to drive his car, so he indulged her. I have a feeling that she demanded the keys because she knew he'd been drinking. It makes more sense. He was probably harassing her while she was driving, and she lost control and wrecked."

"Is it possible he had been drinking and Callie wasn't able to tell?" Honor asked, still unsure about this theory. Would Callie have ridden to the coffee shop with Dawson if he had been drinking. Why would she have been driving down a little country road as fast as they say she was? "Some of the things I'm hearing aren't really adding up with what I know about Callie."

"Vodka doesn't have a strong odor like a lot of alcohol," the policeman said, looking at Honor. "According to his bloodwork, the guy wasn't falling down drunk, at least not if he was used to drinking." He paused and took a bite out of his sugar cookie, a yellow crumb dropping back into the wax paper. "Yeah. It's possible." He wiped another crumb from his mustache. "Do you think the man is telling the truth? Her family said that he's an ex-boyfriend, and that she was not on friendly terms with him."

"No, I definitely think he's lying. He's been following her around for well over a month, practically stalking her. They are not on friendly terms," Honor said, the words coming out in a rush. "There's no way that she was going for a joyride with him. I don't care what he says."

"So, it was like I said." The policeman sipped his coffee again. "She was taking him home, and they got into a fight? That's why she was driving so fast?"

"I'm not sure." Honor's eyes narrowed, his face pinched in frustration. "I don't know what happened, but I do know that Dawson Wallace had been giving her a hard time, and I don't believe a word of that story he's telling."

Clutch laid his hand on Honor's arm and gave him a 'don't lose your cool' look. "Thanks for talking with us," he said to the officer. "I'm sure when Callie wakes up and tells what really happened, it will all make sense." Clutch eased Honor away from the cop and out the doors of the hospital. "I put a sign in the office window while I was out that said we are closed for the rest of the day. Why don't we drive out to the place where she wrecked and check it out? We can grab a chicken strip basket from the gas station and eat on the way."

"Yeah. Let's do that. I'm not hungry, anyway. I want to see his car too. That guy is lying. I'm sure of it."

"He's lying, that's a given," Clutch said. "The question is, why? He's doing it to cover his own skin, but what's going on?"

They pulled into the gas station, and Honor grabbed them something to eat while Clutch put gas in the truck. When Honor got back in the vehicle, he started a group text with Langston Wade and Sydney Madison, letting them know he was going out to see the crash site. He told them what Clutch had found out from Dawson Wallace and the police officer. He did not believe Dawson's story and needed to see the car with his own eyes to try to find the truth. Both men texted back that this was a good idea. Sydney said if they already towed the car, that he could get in touch with the other shop that brought it in. He would make sure they got a look at the car.

Honor put his phone down and picked up a chicken strip from the little paper tray. Clutch headed out of town, following his GPS to Sawmill road. Now that he had a goal, a job to do that would help Callie, Honor was able to think clearer. She would wake up. She had to, and when she did, he would make sure all this mess was cleared up and behind her. She needed to focus on her recovery. He had let her down in the past, but he would die before he let Dawson Wallace weasel his way back into her life—or slander her name.

Ten minutes later, they pulled up to where the accident had happened. The car was gone, already towed away, but the skid marks, shattered glass, and missing bark from the oak tree all told the story of a car flying off the road and colliding with the enormous tree. Across the road on the opposite side, loose hay littered the ground.

"I guess that's where the truck and trailer swerved to miss them," Clutch said, snapping a picture of the skid marks on the road, and then the scattered hay. "The driver must have lost a bale, or part of one, when the trailer hit this ditch."

Another pickup truck pulled onto the shoulder of the road behind Clutch as they made their way down the opposite bank to the tree that had stopped the car's brief flight. "It's a miracle she's still alive," Honor said, touching the light-colored naked flesh of the giant oak where the car had knocked away the bark. Tiny pieces of glass littered the ground at his feet. "This could have." He swallowed the bile rising in his throat. "This could have killed her."

"Paw thought for sure they were dead." A man with sandy blond hair, appearing to be about Honor's age stepped up beside them. His faded jeans, cowboy boots, a baseball cap, and flannel shirt was the same attire as most of the local farmers. "He had to put one of his heart pills under his tongue it upset him so bad."

"Did he see the wreck?" Honor asked, looking at the man. "Has he talked to the police?"

"Paw was driving the tractor," the man said, rubbing the back of his neck. "To be honest, he feels sort of responsible. He was going from my field." He paused and pointed to a gate leading to a hay field a few yards down the road. "To his field less than two miles up the road." He pointed in the opposite direction. "He's been driving that tractor between the two fields since I was a little kid. I've done it too. I told him he wasn't to blame."

"No." Clutch looked up and down the road and then back at the man. "I'm sure he was doing what he always did. We are friends of the girl that was driving the car. She's in ICU and couldn't tell us what happened. We are just trying to figure it all out." He stuck his hand out to the other man. "I'm Clutch Franklin, and this is Honor Jacobs."

"Tom Randall." The man shook Clutch's hand, and then Honor's. "Paw is at his house right up the road if you want to talk to him. The police and the ambulance people tried to get him to go to the hospital, but he wouldn't have none of that. The police are supposed to come talk to him sometime today. They put it off because of the chest pain he was having. He's doing better now. I'm sure he wouldn't mind talking to y'all. Especially if you can tell him how that woman is doing. He was really worried about her."

"He hasn't talked to the police yet?" Honor asked.

"No. When he started having the chest pain, they decided to wait. One of the ambulance drivers is my cousin. He called me, and I came and took Paw home since he wouldn't go to the hospital."

Honor looked at Clutch, then back at Tom Randall. "Yes, if you don't mind, we would like to speak to him."

"Follow me." Tom Randall started back up the side of the ditch onto the road. "He will be relieved to hear that the woman's alive. When he saw the man get out of the car, but the woman didn't, he figured she was dead."

CHAPTER TWENTY-FOUR

*H*onor and Clutch followed Tom Randall through the carport of the little ranch-style brick house and into the homey kitchen. A plump, gray-haired woman in a housedress with an apron tied around her middle turned from the sink where she was washing dishes.

"Maw, these are friends of the woman that was in the wreck." Tom Randall stepped over to the sink and wrapped his arms around his grandmother, giving her a hug. "Do you think Paw is up to talking to them?"

"I guess it will be alright." The woman wiped her damp hands on the front of her apron. "As long as you promise to stop and leave him be if he starts getting upset." She brushed a strand of wavy gray hair away from her face with the back of her hand. "I've never seen Peter that upset in my life. I don't plan on seeing it again anytime soon."

"You just give us the word, and we will stop," Clutch said, smiling down at the woman. "The last thing we want is to bring him grief. Our friend is still unconscious, and we are trying to figure out how all of this happened."

"Alright." The woman's lips pressed into a thin smile.

"Poor girl. I'm praying for her and that young man." She turned and led them through the kitchen into the living room, which was a display of shades of brown. The chestnut paneling from the seventies was shiny clean, with pictures of families posing and smiling through the past few decades scattered on the walls, all in matching brown frames. Across the room, an elderly man in a plaid flannel shirt and overalls sat in a recliner with his feet elevated, his eyes closed. The afternoon sun came through the window and cascaded around the chair, making the man look peaceful, but painfully tired. The woman lead them silently across the brown shag carpet to a green plaid couch and sofa near the recliner. "Have a seat," she whispered. "Let me wake him up."

Clutch and Honor sat on the couch facing the recliner, and Tom sat across from them on the love seat. They watched as the woman placed her hand on the old man's arm.

Peter Randall opened his eyes and smiled up at his wife. "Is it time for coffee?" the old man asked, his gentle eyes searching his wife's face.

"It sure is. And look." The old woman nodded toward the couch. "We have company." Tom introduced Honor and Clutch and explained why they were there.

"If you can tell us what happened," Honor said, smiling politely at the old man, "without it bothering you, we would appreciate it."

"I'm alright now," Peter Randall said, lowering the feet on the recliner. "Just a little shook up. I've given it all to the Lord. That's all I can do." He took a deep breath and stared at his wife's back as she walked to the kitchen.

"I was bringing the tractor from Tom's field to the barn. That black sports car came around me so fast that I didn't have time to pull over and get out of its way. It was doing a hundred, I'm sure." Peter Randall raised his hands, wrinkled with age and leathery from years of working outside. He raked them down the sides of his face, the memory still affecting him. "Paul Sanders was coming around the curve in the opposite lane, pulling a trailer loaded down with hay. The car never slowed. I swerved into the ditch on my side of the road. Paul cut toward me to miss the car, and nearly flipped his trailer before he stopped in the ditch behind me."

Peter Randall turned from the men and stared out the window. A squirrel darted down a nearby oak tree and waited on the roots below, scanning the yard for the dog and other dangers. The old man blinked his eyes, then looked back at Honor and Clutch. "The car never slowed. It missed Paul's truck by inches. The front hit the tree and folded up like an accordion. I've never seen anything like it. I got off my tractor and saw Paul climbing out of his truck. He was already calling 911, so I went across the road. At first nobody moved, and I just knew." He paused and cleared his throat. "I just knew whoever was in that car had to be dead."

Peter Randall's eyes stretched wide as he looked at the men. "It seemed like ten minutes passed, but I guess it couldn't have been too long before that young man climbed out from behind the wheel. He staggered a few feet from the car and fell down. I got to him. He said his girlfriend was still in the car—that she was dead." He rubbed his fingers across his eyes, his voice scratchy with emotion. "I looked in the car. She was covered in blood. Stretched out across the two seats… not moving. I started to pull her out, but you know, you're not supposed to move people unless they are in danger." Peter looked at his grandson, then to Honor and Clutch. "If she had broken her back, I didn't want to make it worse."

"And you stayed with them until the ambulance arrived?" Clutch asked, his voice soft, encouraging. "It sounds like you did the right thing."

Honor listened silently, his forehead creased in a frown. "You said that the man got out on the driver's side?" He finally asked.

"That's right," Peter Randall said, nodding to Honor. "I heard him say that the girl was driving." His gray eyebrows pulled together, and his eyes met Honor's. "I guess he must have crawled over that poor girl to get out of the car if she was driving."

"I guess so," Honor said, his voice flat. "Mr. Randall, is there anything else you can remember that might help us figure out exactly what happened? We appreciate you talking with us."

"I waited there with the man. He kept crying about the woman being dead. Paul came down a few seconds after that and felt her pulse on her neck and told us she wasn't dead. In a little while, the cops and the ambulance got there, but people were already pulling up on the side of the road and seeing if they could help. It turned into a circus pretty quick." He stopped and looked down at his hands, rubbing an old scab on his knuckle, replaying everything that had happened. He raised his tired eyes and stared at Honor. "I guess that's about all I know."

"Mr. Randall." Clutch scratched his cheek. "Did you happen to notice if the passenger's side was bent up so the door wouldn't open?"

"No, it wasn't." Peter Randall looked at Clutch. "A first responder opened it when he got there to check on the woman." He took the cup of coffee from his wife, who had stepped into the room. "I have been so upset that I haven't given it much thought, but I see what you're getting at. I guess the man was so shaken up because he thought his girlfriend was dead that he climbed over her to get out of the car. Didn't do the rational thing like opening his own door."

"I guess so," Clutch said, looking over at Honor. "I guess so."

"Would you two like a cup of coffee?" Peter Randall asked, his face looking more composed. "We have a cup every afternoon around this time. Tom doesn't want our decaffeinated coffee, but it's not too bad once you get used to it."

"No, sir," Honor said, standing from the couch. "I think it's time for us to get going."

"I hope I was some help," the old man said, watching the two men rise. "I imagine the police will be by in a bit. I will be telling them the same thing. I hope it helps you figure this all out." He looked out the window again as the squirrel ran back up the tree and disappeared in the orange and brown leaves. He turned back to the men. "Do you think the girl is going to be okay? She was covered in blood and… so… still."

"Yes, sir." Honor placed his hand on the man's shoulder. "She's tough. It may take a while, but she's going to pull through this." *She has to.*

"What do you think?" Clutch climbed into his truck and looked over at Honor.

"Dawson Wallace was driving that car." Honor's eyes squinted, sharp with anger. "He was driving that car and is trying to put all this off on Callie to cover his sorry, drunk hide."

"I think so too, but I'm not sure what to do about it." Honor started the ignition and put the truck in reverse. "Until Callie wakes up, it's just our word against his. It's like Mr. Randall said. He can claim he was so shaken up that he climbed across her to get out."

"No." Honor pulled his cell phone from his pocket. "Callie was on the passenger's side and he drug her across that console and into the driver's seat. I know that's what happened. We'll prove it." He punched in a text to Sydney and Langston. "We won't stop until we do. If Callie can't walk, or has injuries caused by him moving her, he better hope the police throw him in jail." Honor dropped the cell phone in his lap and looked out the front window. "That will be the only place he will be safe from me."

"I know you're mad." Clutch pulled down the gravel driveway and stopped before pulling onto Sawmill road. "I'm mad too. But you can't let it get the best of you. If you do something dumb, like hurt this man, or whatever you have planned, you'll only be bringing more drama and pain into Callie's life." He reached over and squeezed Honor's shoulder, then pulled onto the road. "The last thing she needs is to wake up and find out you're in jail for assaulting her ex-boyfriend."

"Yeah." Honor rubbed his hand across the back of his neck. "You're right. I'm not sure how to deal with all this. I mean, I know what we need to do with." He raised his hand and pointed in the direction of the crash site. "That. I don't know what to do with all this anger and hatred that it's causing inside me."

"You have to have faith."

"Faith? In God?" Anger pinched Honor's face as the bitter words flowed. "Because my faith in our justice system has slipped a notch or two over the past few hours. The cops should have already talked to that old man, should have investigated all of this immediately. If Callie dies, they should charge Dawson Wallace with manslaughter. But he's going to lie his way out of this."

"Yes." Clutch pulled over on the side of the road and put the truck back in park. "Yes. Faith in God. That's exactly what I'm talking about. You think figuring all of this out is on you, that you're the only one that can do this the right way." His lips turned down, and he rubbed his eyelid. "Look. I'm your best friend, so I can tell you this. Even though you are usually the smartest guy in the room, you are not the only smart guy in the room. I'm afraid that being so smart sometimes keeps you from giving things to God. You think you can do it all yourself. You can't." Clutch waited, staring at Honor's face as he processed what he was being told. "God is in control, Honor, not you. You need to have faith that he will bring justice to his daughter. Let him use you, be a tool in his hands. If not, the anger will take control and you won't be doing anybody any good, especially Callie."

"That's harsh."

"That's the truth." Clutch smiled and looked down at Honor's phone, vibrating with a new text. "Sometimes you need to be smacked in the face with a little dose of truth. It's for your own good, and I'm the one to do it. Don't waste your anger on the police, and don't go off half-cocked." He watched Honor pick up his phone and read the message. "Now. What next?"

CHAPTER TWENTY-FIVE

*A*fter Clutch pulled back onto the road, Honor gave him the address for the garage where the police towed Dawson Wallace's Mustang. The ride to the enormous garage had been quiet. Honor spent the time in thought contemplating what Clutch said. Clutch was right. He couldn't take the law into his own hands, but he still needed to do what was in his power to make things right for Callie. She deserved better than what he had been.

They pulled into an enormous lot overflowing with wrecked vehicles, and Honor's eyes searched what resembled a junk yard more than a mechanic's garage. "I don't see it," he said, stepping out of the truck.

"Me neither, but as crowded and unorganized as this place is, it could still be out there." Honor walked around his truck. "Come on. Let's go inside and ask somebody about it. We'll waste all day trying to find it out here on our own."

They weeded their way through the vehicular carnage and finally made it to the garage. The interior of the garage was as neat as the yard was messy, with the two doors rolled up in the back of the building to bring the tow truck in and out. Honor looked over near the wall, his eyes adjusting to the dimmer light. The Mustang, its shattered windshield, the safety glass smashed into thousands of tiny pieces, its crumpled body barely resembling a car sat waiting to be examined. His stomach burned as he took in the wreckage. *Thank you, God, for bringing her through this.*

A humbling wave of regret washed over Honor. Clutch was right, as usual. His pride had kept him from talking to Callie in the first place. He thought he was better, smarter, even closer to God than Callie. That's why he had not asked her about her past. Worse yet, that's why he had not prayed about how to handle it when he found out about her abortion.

Now. Now he was doing it again. He stared at the wreck, the sick knot in his stomach growing. The front of the car was annihilated, crushed almost up to the windshield. The impact had pushed up the roof, and the cab had tried to buckle. The back glass and side windows were cracked with hunks missing. How had she survived? How had either of them survived?

Honor looked around the garage. He was alone. Clutch must have gone into the little store or office or whatever the other part of the building was to talk to the owner. He stepped closer to the car and looked at the dried blood on the passenger's side of the windshield. That was where Callie hit her head. The airbag had deployed on the driver's side and its dust was all over the dash, or what was left of the dash. He leaned in and looked at the floorboard under the blood stain. Callie's purse. One of Callie's shoes.

God. Please forgive me for trying to do this... trying to do everything without you. Forgive my pride, Lord. I have been so eaten up with pride for so long that I didn't even realize it was controlling me. God, please. Honor opened his eyes and stared at the wreckage, fear of what might have happened catching in his throat. *God, thank you for not taking Callie, for giving me another chance with her. Please use me as you see fit to find out what really happened. And please, please heal her, God.*

He pulled out his phone and snapped pictures of the car, of everything he saw. He didn't know, nor did he understand why Callie had gotten in the car with Dawson Wallace in the first place, but it didn't matter. All that mattered was that she was in that hospital being accused by that scum ex-boyfriend of crashing this car. She was unable to defend herself against him, but Honor could, and he would. He wouldn't take the law into his own hands, but he would show them what he found out. He wouldn't render out the punishment on Dawson Wallace that he deserved. He had to leave that to God—like Clutch said.

Honor walked around to the driver's side of the car and looked at the seat. The door was open and glass from the car door littered the interior. Broken bottles, vodka bottles, were scattered in the back. Honor squatted down and looked at the floorboard under the steering wheel. Another vodka bottle lay near the gas pedal. He looked under the edge of the seat where it had probably been hidden. Yeah. Dawson was driving, no doubt. His brow furrowed as he stared at the seat. It was set all the way back, way too far for Callie's petite height. Way farther than the passenger's seat.

Honor snapped some more pictures. He had what he needed. Callie hadn't been driving, and now he could prove it. He looked around the garage again. They needed to get these photos to the police station. The sooner he showed these pictures to the authorities, the sooner they could confront Dawson and get the truth from him.

Floating. That's what she was doing, and it was nice. Every once in a while, she would hear voices, feel something, something unpleasant. Then a cool rush would go through her arm, and she would float some more. The voices were louder now. Fiona's, Sidney's, some familiar voices she should know, mingled with those of her sister and brother. She tilted her head back, trying to push above the clouds, but something prevented the movement and it—it hurt. A moan escaped, and she pushed again, this time not with her head. That effort had drained her. This time, she pushed her eyelids.

The clouds she was floating in started to drift apart as the pain, sharp and throbbing at the forefront, aching and soreness piled in the background, weighed down on her. Go back to floating. She could do that, leave the voices alone, but something wasn't right. She pushed against the stabbing pain and a slit of harsh, blaring, white light broke through.

"Fi?" Was that her voice? It sounded more like a toad.

"Callie."

She moved her eyes. Whatever was pushing against her chin wouldn't let her move her head. "Fi. Something's on my neck."

"Oh, Callie." Fiona's voice cracked with emotion as Callie turned her eyes toward her sister's voice. "Callie, I'm right here with Sidney and Langston and Adelyn and Honor," Fi said, tears dripping down her face. "We're all right here, honey. Happy Thanksgiving."

"Honor?" Callie searched Fiona's face. Why was she hurting? Why couldn't she turn her head? Why was everyone staring at her? Her eyes left Fiona and traveled down the line of people scrunched at her bedside. "Duck." She was still croaking. "Duck, I messed up." She raised her hand. It hurt. "Duck."

Honor stepped up closer to the head of the bed, toward the hand that was reaching out to him. The rest of the family shuffled away, making room for him to reach her. "Callie." Honor swallowed, his eyes wide with fear, hope, sadness. He placed his hand under Callie's, and she lowered her hand back to the bed, into his palm. When their hands touched, Honor stared down into her eyes nestled in bruised, swollen sockets. Leaning closer, his lips almost touched her face. "You're going to be alright, Callie. Don't talk. You're still too weak."

"Don't leave me, Duck."

"I'm not, Callie… I'm never going to leave." A tear trickled down Honor's face and dropped onto the bedcovers. "I'm here with you, always. Don't worry."

Ugh. What is happening to me? Callie opened her eyes. It was easier this time. At least there was that. Flashes and pictures bounced around in her head as she tried to put her brain back in order. The wreck. All of that horrible day had come flooding back in a rush some time ago. She wasn't sure when. Time, and keeping up with it, was a problem. She had opened her eyes several times, at least she thought she had. She'd said a few things, she wasn't sure what, and listened to her family. And Duck. She turned her head to the nurse at her bedside. No Duck. "Ow." She looked down at her hand, red and puffy.

"I replaced your IV. See?" The nurse pointed to where she had connected a tube to something she had screwed into her skin. "The old one infiltrated." The nurse lifted Callie's hand and showed her the redness Callie had already noticed. "I can put some ice on that. Keep it elevated on the pillow here, and it will feel better in a bit," the nurse said, laying Callie's hand back down.

"How long have I been here?" Callie flexed the fingers in her swollen hand the nurse had been working on, and then her other hand. She looked at the other hand as a sharp pain ran up her arm. A cast from her elbow to her palm held the limb prisoner except for an open area for her thumb. "I broke my arm."

"Eight days, and yes, your arm is broken." The nurse's eyes sparkled, and she smiled at Callie. "I believe you are coming around to the land of the living. A lot of people have been praying for you."

Callie ran her tongue along the roof of her dry mouth. Something hard was in the back of her throat. She reached up with the IV hand and touched a skinny tube taped to her face, going through her nose and down the back of her throat.

"Don't pull that. That's how we've been feeding you." The nurse took Callie's hand and guided it back to the bed. "You have been asleep for quite a while. You've woken up three or four times for a couple of seconds over the past few days, but I think you may actually be going to come out of it this time. If you are up to it, and stay awake, the doctor has ordered a swallowing test. If you pass, we can pull that tube from your nose."

Callie nodded and reached up, brushing her fingers along her neck. The skin was tender, sore to the touch. She ran her fingers across to her collarbone on the side with the broken arm. A sharp pain radiated up and down when she pressed the area. "It hurts over here."

"You have a broken collarbone. Do you need something for pain?"

"Will it make me sleep?" Callie winced and lowered her hand, tired from the simple movement.

"Yes, but if you need it, take the medication. We can wait to test your swallowing when you wake up."

"No." Callie rubbed her tongue around again, feeling the gooey dry interior of her mouth. "I'm fine. Can I have my phone?" She shifted her shoulders and grimaced. Everything was sore. "I need to call Du—Honor. Honor Jacobs."

"I'm not sure about your phone. It wasn't on you when you came up here, but you had surgery to set that arm after you came through the emergency room. They may have locked it away somewhere in the hospital. Don't worry though. Honor is waiting to come in. I told him I would get him as soon as we finished your bath."

"Bath?" Callie looked down, wiggling her toes. "How are we going to do that? I'm not sure I can stand up."

"No, no standing yet, but that's very good." The nurse smiled, watching Callie's movements under the covers. "Can you pull your knees up?" She waited as Callie did as asked. "The doctor is going to be extremely pleased with you today."

"How am I going to take a bath?" Callie stared at the nurse as she jotted something on a piece of paper. She needed to hurry up. Honor was waiting. The nurse looked at the monitors behind Callie's head and continued to write. "The bath?" Callie asked again, impatience in her voice.

"I have already given you your bath." The nurse folded the paper and slipped it in her pocket. "Changed your bed, emptied your catheter, and changed your dressing and your IV. You are good to go."

How did she sleep through all of that? No wonder she couldn't keep up with time. She looked as the nurse pull the pale-yellow curtain from around the bed, revealing a compact hospital room with glass walls. "Oh. This is so weird."

"I am sure it is." The nurse stepped to the glass door and leaned on it with her shoulder. "But I think today is the day that you start getting things back to normal. Why, look at you." Her eyes crinkled with a smile. "The brain is an amazing thing. You went from our not knowing if you would wake up, to carrying on complete conversations in a few short minutes. I'm glad I was the nurse on duty to see you come out of it. You are on the mend." She glanced around the room and pushed the door open with her shoulder. "Can I get you anything before I call the doctor?"

"Du—I mean Honor."

"One Duck coming up."

CHAPTER TWENTY-SIX

"*Y*ou look thin." Callie's eyes roamed across Honor's face, her heart doing a flip-flop. He stepped through the glass door, and a longing tugged from deep within her. His jaw was scruffy with black whiskers and his cheekbones were more prominent than the last time she saw him. The day she had walked out of the office. It seemed like decades ago.

"You look beautiful." Honor stepped over to the bed, his voice deep. He opened his mouth to say something else, but closed it again. He eased his hand from behind his back and held out his gift.

Callie adjusted her shoulders on the pillows. The nurse had raised the head of the bed to a sitting position before she stepped out earlier, and it seemed odd. She was still trying to find the most comfortable way to sit on her bruises after being flat on her back for so long.

Laughter bubbled from her as Honor drew near. "Ooh." She touched her hands to her ribs. "That hurt." Tears filled her eyes even though her mouth drew into a broad smile, the cracks in her dry lips causing her to wince. "Oh, Duck. I love it." She reached up and took the feathery soft stuffed animal, a golden-yellow baby duck, from his hands. She snuggled the plush stuffed toy, about the size of a throw pillow, to her chest. "A duck from my Duck." She left the present on her chest and patted the side of the bed. "Sit down." She cleared her dry, scratchy throat, trying to ignore the tube running down the back of her mouth. "I want to talk to you about what happened."

Honor eased onto the edge of the bed, careful not to bump her, or the tubes above and under the covers. "Okay, but the nurse said I couldn't wear you out. You don't need to overdo it."

"Posh," Callie snorted. "I feel like I've been in this bed one hundred years." Her hand reached up and stroked the softness of the yellow duck on her chest. "It's so weird. I feel like I've been here forever, but I can't even remember how I got in this room." Her eyes wandered around, taking in the monitors and IV poles with bags of fluids hanging by the bed. "The nurse said it's been eight days."

"That's right." Honor shifted his hip on the bed. "Today is December first. You slept through Thanksgiving, but don't worry. We decided that when you get out of here, we will have a do over."

"We? Did you go to Fiona's to eat with my family?" Callie frowned. "Aww. I missed my banana pudding lesson with Mrs. Albertson."

"No. I didn't go anywhere but here for Thanksgiving, but your family made me a plate and dropped it by my house that evening." Honor reached up and touched the stuffed duck on Callie's chest. "You woke up for a few seconds that day, but went right back out. Do you remember that?"

"No. Honestly, the last thing I remember is being in the car, telling Dawson to slow down. I remember seeing that old man on that tractor, and then. Nothing else. Until today."

"Do you remember everything?" Honor turned his eyes from Callie's swollen and bruised hand on the stuffed animal to her purple, swollen eyes, the whites peeking out of the slits as she watched him. "Everything before the wreck?"

"Yes." Callie scrutinized Honor's face, something strange shadowed his eyes. "Honor, I need to tell you some things. There are some things about me…"

"Callie." Honor reached up and gently pushed a tangled strand of blond hair away from her bruised and swollen face. "You don't have to tell me anything." He sucked in a breath of air. "I don't care about any of that. All I care about is you, and you getting well."

"No." Callie captured Honor's hand in hers and held it, drawing it down to her side. "Honor, I'm not who you think I am." She swallowed and coughed, then winced. *Stupid tube. Stupid collarbone. Stupid ribs.* "I mean. I am who you think I am now. But while you were away." A tear squeezed out of the corner of her eye and ran down her face, over her lips. "I was sort of wild. If you ask some of the people I went to college with, they will never believe that I'm a Christian now."

"Callie. It's okay." Honor's fingertip stroked her hand, his touch gentle, his eyes piercing hers. "I know. I don't agree with what you did, but it's not who you are now." His gaze cut away to the duck, the child's toy sitting on her chest. "Our beliefs about abortion aren't the same, but we will work through that. I won't let that come between us. I." He looked back up, searching her face. "I think I." He paused, the shake of his head barely visible. "I know I love you. Nothing that you've done or ever will do can change that."

"I love you too." The words came out as a sob. Callie leaned forward off the pillows toward Honor, his caring face, his tender eyes. "Duck, I need to tell you." She pulled in a deep breath and started coughing, pulling the stuffed animal tight to her, splinting her ribs. She fell back on the pillows and gasped at the sharp pain.

"Let me get the nurse." Honor's eye stretched wide, and he stood up from the side of the bed. "Don't talk, Callie. Just breathe."

The nurse stepped into the room from the glass door behind Honor. "Okay, young lady. It's time for you to rest." She stepped over to the bed and picked up a tube from the bedside table. "Here. Let's put your oxygen back on for a few minutes."

The coughing eased, and Callie's brow furrowed. *Ugg. So frustrating. I can't even talk without my body throwing a hissy fit.* "I'm okay now," she said, her words coming out in little puffs.

"No." The nurse shook a finger at Callie and then turned to Honor. "That's enough for now. The speech therapist will be here shortly to check her swallowing. If that goes well, then we will pull that tube from her nose and let her have some ice chips. She has had a busy day. Come back this afternoon."

"Honor." Callie looked past the nurse where Honor stood, his posture rigid with worry. "I love you. I'm fine. I promise."

It had been a brutal morning, but things were looking up. The speech therapist had given her a passing grade with her swallowing, and the nurse had pulled the nasogastric tube from her nose. Apparently, her gag reflex was alive and well. When the tip of the tube ran across the back of her throat, she had gagged and vomited up the milky feeding she had been receiving to keep her going. Heaving with cracked ribs was no walk in the park, but she had made it through, distracted by what Honor had told her earlier. What had he meant?

She had gobbled up the ice the nurse passed out in stingy little helpings with no further nausea. After an eternity, she had moved on to sips of ice water. That had been heaven. She would not love any Christmas gift she would receive later that month more than that first little Styrofoam cup of ice water.

Through all of that, and now the physical therapist helping her move from the bed to the nearby chair, her thoughts had gone over and over what Honor said. He loved her. A flush of warmth filled her body. They could work out the rest as long as he loved her. But what was the rest? Who talked to him, and what did he know? Fiona wouldn't have told him about the baby without talking to her first. A trickle of fear ran down her spine. Dawson. Dawson must have told him about the baby, and if he told him, then Honor believed Callie had an abortion. The conversation from that morning played over in her mind. Yes, that was the only thing that made sense. Honor thought she had sacrificed the life of her unborn baby to continue her own reckless lifestyle.

But he loves me anyway. Callie looked down at the side of the chair for the call light. She had to talk to him, had to get things straight. She pushed the button again and again and again. *Where is that nurse?*

"You ready to get back in bed, sunshine?" The nurse stepped up to the chair and took the call light from Callie's hand, as she released her thumb from the button. "You are doing remarkably well. I have a feeling we will be pulling that catheter from your bladder and moving you to a regular room either this evening or in the morning."

"Yes. I'm ready to get back in bed." Callie watched the nurse lift the blanket from her legs and move the little bag with her urine, *yuck,* from where it was hooked to the side of her chair to the bedside, a foot away. "That's not what I wanted, though. I need to see Honor Jacobs. When can he come back in?"

"Well, look at you. I heard you were up and about." A tall, thin man with salt and pepper gray hair cut short and neat walked into the room. "How are you doing with the water and ice?"

"Fine." Callie stood, the nurse's arms around her, ignoring the dizziness as they pivoted her from the bed to the chair. "The water was great." She waited while the nurse straightened the covers over her lower half, then looked at the doctor, who stepped up to her bed. He leaned over and pried open her eyelids, shining a penlight on her pupils. The pressure of his fingers forcing her lids up hurt like the dickens, but she ground her teeth together. She would not have another coughing fit. "Who are you?" She asked when he finally stood back up straight.

"I'm Dr. Stanford, your neurologist. It appears you are going to pull through this fine." He turned to the nurse at his side. "Do another MRI and CAT scan, but if all of that is good, she can move to a regular room if the ortho and the rest agree." The nurse nodded and jotted something down on her little paper.

"When can I go home?"

"I'm not sure, but if you make as much progress tomorrow as you did today, it won't be long."

The doctor turned on his heels and left the room without another word. Callie frowned. Bedside manner was not his strong suit. She watched the glass door shut behind him, then looked over to the little sink. The nurse had pulled the yellow curtain hanging from the ceiling around that side of her bed for most of the day, and she had not noticed it before. Her eyes traveled up from the sink to the mirror above it. A wave of nausea washed over her, her throat tightening with tension. Was that her? Her eyes were swollen slits. The swelling across her nose made it resemble a purple blob. Her forehead was wrapped in a bandage, and her lips were puffy and cracked, crusted with patches of dried blood. Her entire face was shades of purple and green, with tiny patches of white filling in the cracks.

I could have died. She knew the wreck had banged her up, but—this? Was Dawson dead? She was mad at him, didn't like him, didn't want to be around him, but she didn't want him dead. A sudden weight pushed on her shoulders, and she dropped her head back on the pillows, the fight in her draining away. *Oh, God. I'm so sorry for hating that man. I lift him up to you, God. I pray that you change his heart. He needs you, God, just like I did. Just like I do, Father. Thank you for... for letting me have more time here. For remaining with me through all my clumsy stupidity.*

Callie's eyes remained closed. She needed to talk to Honor, to get things straight. She needed to check on Dawson. She was so tired. Her thoughts drifted away as her body relaxed. Rest. All those troubles would wait. She needed rest. The clouds closed back over her, and she let herself be engulfed back down to where all her problems, all the aches and pain were gone.

CHAPTER TWENTY-SEVEN

*W*hat kind of man gave the woman he loved a stuffed duck? Honor glanced down at his watch. It had been four hours. He had run back to his office to check on things after he left Callie earlier. Clutch had everything under control and was getting ready to go do a presentation in an adjoining parish. The Christmas bonus in Clutch's envelope this year would be huge. His friend was picking up the slack without being asked, while Honor divided his time between the hospital and the office.

He stepped off the elevator and took his usual seat in the ICU waiting room. Fiona and Langston would be there shortly. They came by every afternoon, and Sidney and Adeline were there early every morning. They were all thrilled when he texted them that Callie was awake and talking. The last eight days had been brutal on her family and him.

Talking. They needed to do that, but not at the expense of her health. He looked down at the flowers in his hands, a bright mixture of every color under the sun. At first he had asked the florist for roses, but then remembered the bouquet she received on her first day at work. From Dawson. He didn't want to bring back that day to her or remind her of that guy in any way.

His first gift was a pack of instant oatmeal, the second a stuffed duck. No wonder Callie had never seen him as boyfriend material. That was all changing now. She said she loved him. That was all that mattered. He would buy her flowers every day, drown her in oatmeal, do whatever it took to make her smile. To show her how much he cared.

He looked at his cell phone again. The nurse should be coming out to let visitors through any minute now. He tapped the icon on the screen and looked at the pictures of the car. The officer at the police station had listened to Honor and Clutch when they took the pictures by the station last week. The process had seemed incredibly slow, but over the next couple of days, the law talked to Mr. Randall, looked at the car, and finally talked to Dawson Wallace again. According to the cop that Honor had come to know through all of this, Dawson had broken down and sobbed like a baby. Not because he lied about Callie, endangered her life, nearly killed her. He cried because the DUI and whatever would go along with it related to the crash would make him lose his scholarship to the University of Texas. Honor tapped the screen, closing the pictures. He was praying about his attitude with the man, but if he never saw him again, it wouldn't bother him in the least.

A rush of cool air hit him, and he looked up at the nurse, waiting for him to go in. He stood and held the flowers in front of him like a shield. *Lord, give me the words to explain to her how much she means to me.*

"Those are for me?" Callie looked at the beautiful bouquet in Honor's hands. Her heart swelled as her gaze traveled up to the man she loved. Her eyes pulled away from his beautiful face to her reflection in the nearby mirror. She closed her eyes. "Can you pull that curtain over a little?"

"Sure." Honor tugged on the curtain at the foot of the bed, drawing it across to the other side. "I'm trying to up my game on the gift giving thing," he said, laying the flowers on the bedside table near the stuffed animal from before.

"They're lovely, and so is my duck. Don't ever change what your heart tells you to give me." Callie choked back a sob and looked at Honor, at his dark hair, green eyes behind black lashes, his square jawline, and full lips. He was so handsome. How come she hadn't really recognized it before? "Honor, I'm all messed up—hard to look at. You don't have to come back if you, you know." She ducked her chin down, the hair tucked over her shoulders falling over her battered face. "If you don't want to look at me like this."

"Like what?" Honor leaned forward and gently placed a finger under Callie's chin, lifting up her beautiful face. "Like someone so brave, so strong? Someone that I am so grateful to have in my life?" He lifted the hair near her face and placed it back over her shoulder. "Callie, wounds heal, bruises fade. You are in there, and it's you I love. I don't care about how you look."

"What if I look different?" Callie ran her tongue out over her lips, thickly coated with Vaseline. "There is a cut on my forehead under that bandage and look." She lifted her hand to her swollen and discolored nose. "See that? That's stitches. So are those over my eyebrow. What if I have scars? Scars that don't go away?"

Honor leaned in and pulled her to his chest, his lips touching the top of her head. "Callie, you will always be beautiful to me. You're beautiful now, and you will be beautiful when we're in our nineties, surrounded by grandkids and great grandkids."

"I didn't have an abortion."

"I told you it doesn't matter." Honor lifted his hand to stroke her back, but stopped, afraid of hurting her. "Dawson told me what happened with you and him. I didn't handle it well." He bent his head down and touched his lips to the top of her head again. "I'm so sorry about that. If I would have talked to you about this that night of the party. If I'd confronted Dawson instead of acting like I was above all of that, this never would have happened. I was a jerk again after he told me about you and him and the pregnancy. I'm sorry I didn't help you handle all of this."

"It wasn't your problem, Duck."

"But it should have been." Honor pulled back and looked down at Callie. "You are my friend and even more than that. I have known I've had powerful feelings for you for quite a while. Known I was falling in love with you. I should have been by your side, not pouting and acting like a jerk while you were dealing with a boyfriend who needed his…. Well, you know."

"Honor." Callie reached her hand up and stroked his cheek. "I don't know what he told you, but when I found out I was pregnant, I went to him. I was scared, terrified, really. I thought I loved him and that he loved me too. I figured he would marry me." Her fingers drew down across his cheek toward his chin. "He said he would give me money for an abortion. I was floored, and I broke up with him that very day. Looking back, I can see that it took that shock to make me get my life back on track. I buckled down with my classes and decided I would have the baby and raise him or her on my own. I didn't want a man who didn't want our child, but I wanted the baby. No matter what I had to give up or sacrifice to keep my baby, I was going to do it."

"What happened? Did you decide to put the baby up for adoption?"

"No." Callie's eyes searched Honors, willing him to believe her. "When I was around three months pregnant, I miscarried." She pulled her hand down. "I've felt so guilty. Like God was punishing me, but then, on that Saturday, I told Fiona. She talked to me about Jesus and how he had given up everything just to make me his, how he loved me, even when I was stupid. He wouldn't take my baby just to spite me."

"No." Honor reached down and picked up Callie's hand, bringing it back to his face. He wanted to kiss her, press his lips to hers, but he was scared he would hurt her. "God only wants good for you. God has brought something good out of your tragedy, Callie. That's what he does. When we surrender our ugly mess, he takes it and makes something beautiful." He touched her fingers to his lips, kissing the tips. "He brought you to me."

EPILOGUE

"Is the train straight?" Callie looked over her shoulder at the lace flowing behind her. She watched Fiona reach down and move a corner of the gauzy white material. "I still can't believe this is happening."

"It's happening alright," Fiona said, standing back up and stepping beside her. She placed a bouquet of spring flowers and baby's breath in Callie's hands. "And you are going to be late for your own wedding if you don't get out there."

"I am so blessed. I still can't believe this is all for real." Callie waited while Fiona lifted her veil from her shoulders and pulled it in place over her face. She looked in the mirror hanging on the wall in the little Sunday School room in the back of the church. Apparently, the room where the old men met each week also doubled as the bridal room for weddings. She leaned in closer, looking at the slight scar above her left eyebrow, almost hidden with her makeup. The scar on her nose had faded last year, shortly after the doctor removed the stitches.

The gash over her eye had been deeper, leaving a faint pink line—barely noticeable. The other scar, the one on her forehead, she would have forever to remind her. She looked at the thin pucker behind her wisp of bangs. That line would always remind her that last December, Honor Jacobs had pledged his life to her through the good, the bad, and the ugly.

When she came out of the hospital, a week after their talk had straightened things out, he brought her a ring. "I don't want to rush you. We can stay engaged for a decade if that's what you need. I just have to know that you want this, too. That you want to spend your life with me, bring a family into this world with me, grow old and die with me."

The decision had not been hard. It didn't matter if she was in Carson's Bayou or Baton Rouge or Indonesia. She no longer cared, as long as Honor was by her side. They decided on a June wedding, eighteen months down the road.

When the doctors discharged her from the hospital, she moved in with Fiona and Langston. Under her sister's meticulous care, the time flew by as her wounds and bones healed. After two months, she started to feel smothered and insisted she needed to get back to her own place. She was ready to return to work and live a normal life.

As the couple spent more time together, as their relationship kept growing, the wedding date seemed a decade away. At Thanksgiving, Callie presented the family with her now famous banana pudding, courtesy of Mrs. Albertson's recipe, and a couple of happy lessons in the old lady's kitchen. "Honor and I have an announcement."

Honor stood beside Callie, taking her hand in his. "We have decided that we can't wait until next summer to get married," he said, looking around the table of expectant faces. "We are having a small ceremony at our church on December first."

"The anniversary of my waking up seemed like an appropriate day," Callie said, leaning over and kissing Honor on the cheek. "It really is the day Duck became mine after all."

Callie blinked her eyes, pushing back the happy memory to focus on the joys ahead. She followed Fiona and Adelyn from the Sunday school room to the back foyer of the church. Sydney stood there, looking handsome, but a bit uncomfortable in a black suit, waiting to walk her down the aisle. She peered through the veil to the front of the church where Honor waited, Clutch faithfully at his side. It had been a long journey. Everything she ever really wanted was right here in Carson's Bayou after all. She traveled out of town on business with Honor often, but her life, the life she wanted for her family, was right here in this small town with these people, her family and friends. Life was good. So was Carson's Bayou.

If you enjoyed this book, please take a few minutes to leave a review now. Authors, myself included, really appreciate this, and it helps draw more readers to books they may enjoy as well. Thanks! KC

Join KC's Newsletter to receive an eBook copy of Music Smarts and Humble Hearts

Please keep reading for a sneak peek at Kid Smarts and Wistful Hearts, coming early 2023.

KID SMARTS AND WISTFUL HEARTS

CHAPTER ONE

"You're ugly." Bailey Lewis glared at her big brother, her five-year-old chin firm with stubborn indignation.

"Dad." Scout Lewis shouted through the living room toward the kitchen as he threw down his little sister's tennis shoe. No answer. "You can go to school barefoot, for all I care." He stomped into the bathroom and slammed the door, listening as the expected screams and sobs of his little sister filled the house.

"Scout." Drake Lewis's voice called over Bailey's continued shrieks, almost vibrating the bathroom door. "What's wrong with your sister?"

Scout kept putting the toothpaste on his brush, ignoring the cacophony of sound beyond the sanctity of the locked door. Gracie always managed to disappear when Bailey needed something done. Today Scout was following her example.

"What's the matter, squirt?" Drake walked into the living room, wiping his damp hands on a kitchen towel. "You sound like somebody chopped off your big toe." He stepped over to where his youngest daughter continued to sob, her unruly mass of tight blond curls sticking out in every direction, so much like her mother's that it made Drake's heart ache. "Hey, hey, hey." He sat down on the couch and pulled the five-year-old into his lap. "All that cat-a-walling's not helping anything. Take a breath and tell me what's going on."

"Scout said I was a baby." Bailey wiped the back of her hand across her drippy nose and looked up at her daddy with deep blue eyes fringed with surprisingly dark lashes. "He said I needed baby shoes that babies could put on until I could learn to tie my own."

Drake picked up the tail of his t-shirt and wiped his youngest child's snotty nose. It had started running Saturday evening after the kids came back from his momma's. He heard her coughing several times throughout the night. He laid his hand on her forehead. "You're a little warm." He leaned over and picked up her shoe. He was off from the hardware store today since he worked Saturday, but he was supposed to check the plumbing over at a house in the garden district. Maybe Momma could watch her today. He would give her some Tylenol with her breakfast.

Bailey let out a barking cough as he slipped on her shoe and tied the laces. No, she needed to go to the clinic. He would have to take her in, then go do the plumbing job later. "How does skipping school sound today? You can hang out with me, then go see Mawmaw after while?"

The crying that sounded like the child was going through irreparable emotional damage stopped so suddenly that the quiet pounded in Drake's ears. "Good. I don't like school. I'm smart without it. Mawmaw says so."

"Well, you have to learn to read. How are you going to come work at the hardware store with me if you don't learn to read?" He stood, hoisting the child up on his hip. "Where's your brother and sister? We need to eat breakfast and hit the road or they're going to be late for school again."

"Scout's in the bathroom and Gracie went outside to check on Rambler."

Drake shook his head as he walked over to the window and looked out at the frost and mist on the icy cold February ground. Gracie, his seven-year-old, squatted barefoot in the grass in her flannel nightgown, looking under Drake's truck. He dropped Bailey down to the floor and stepped toward his front door. "Go get in your chair and pick out which biscuit you want."

He opened his front door and freezing winter air gushed into the living room. "Gracie Nell Lewis, get in this house right now." His voice bellowed across the yard loud enough to wake the neighbors. It didn't matter. Momma's house was up the hill. Quin, his little brother, lived in the double-wide across the road, and his older brother Hank lived on his other side, but he was never home, anyway. Everybody was used to his yelling.

Gracie stood and looked over her shoulder at her father, not the least bit worried by his fierce tone. She slowly moped back to the front porch, the frosty ground crunching under her feet. Rambler, Quin's mutt of the Heinze-Fifty-Seven variety, had been the topic of a heated discussion last night before bedtime. When Quin was home from offshore, the dog stayed across the road where he belonged, but Quin, being Quin, didn't bother with what happened to the animal while he was out on his hitch. Drake had come in to tell the girls goodnight and found the ancient dog piled up in the bed with Gracie, fleas and all.

"Daddy, he'll freeze tonight. I promised Uncle Quin I'd take care of Rambler when he was gone. He gave me five dollars to put food in his bowl every day."

"I don't care if he gave you a gold monkey. That old dog is

not sleeping in your bed. He can go sleep in Mawmaw's shed with Poochie and be just fine."

"But he's my responsibility, Dad." Gracie's eyes had teared up as she wrapped her arms around the slobbery old hound. "He needs me."

Quin. I'm going to skin you alive. "He's not your responsibility. He's Uncle Quin's." He reached down and pulled the dog from the bed onto the floor. "Besides, Poochie needs Rambler to snuggle to tonight to keep her warm."

"Mawmaw said Poochie needs to stay away from Rambler or some baby Poochie's will be showing up soon."

"Don't you worry about Poochie and Rambler." Drake kissed his middle child, her sandy brown hair so much like his at her age falling into her eyes. "Mawmaw and Uncle Quin need to learn how to take care of their dog's business and they wouldn't have those problems."

He reached down and put his hand on Gracie's back, hustling her into the living room. How come she could practically run around buck-naked in the dead of winter and never get a sniffle while Bailey seemed to be sick every time he turned around? "You're as cold as a frog, Gracie, and you smell like a dog. Go wash up. We're going to be late again."

Drake nudged his middle daughter in the direction of the bathroom and stepped into the hallway to hunt for Scout. It wasn't like him to not be in the thick of things, ordering his sisters around and trying to take on the role of man of the house. His son's bedroom door was cracked open and Drake stuck his head in the door, but stopped at what he saw. Scout, his coat on and his schoolbag on his back, was kneeling by his bed, his eyes closed.

"God, I'm doing what I can to help Daddy, but sometimes I'm not enough."

Drake's eyes filled with compassion as his son's prayer filled his heart.

"Daddy is trying, but sometimes he gets mad because things don't go right. So, God, I was wondering if you could bring Daddy a wife. He tries to act like he don't need one, but I can tell he does. I figured if I could tell, then God, you can tell too. That's all I'm asking for, God." Scout pulled his hands down from where they were folded in prayer, but pushed them back up. "And I'm really sorry for being mean to Bailey this morning, but you know she started it. Amen."

***

Esther pulled her thick mane of caramel colored curls back in a loose ponytail at the nape of her neck. The sudden drop in temperature from the sixties last week to the thirties over the weekend had brought in a flood of the routine asthmatics, along with several more kids with signs of respiratory infections. A few children had tested positive for strep, but thankfully they hadn't seen any positive for influenza.

She washed her hands as she stared into the bathroom mirror. Her lips were still a little chapped from being out in the wind over the weekend, helping her twin brother Barlow make sure their pipes were wrapped well enough against the freeze. She tugged down the gray scrub top over her middle and tossed the damp paper towels in the trash. The suit was getting a little snug, but it was still okay to wear. She hadn't gotten on the scales but could tell she'd put on about ten pounds over the past three months. She was built just like her mother and most of the women in her family, short with plenty of curves. The ten pounds were what Granny referred to as her winter coat. She would probably drop them again when spring arrived, and she started playing softball with the ladies at the church. Then again, she was turning thirty next month. This fuller look might be her new normal. If it was, that would be okay, too.

"Esther, the Lewis kid is in room four," Sandy, the med tech, said as they stepped up to the nurse's desk.

"Which one?" Esther looked down at the never-ending flow of charts. She had hoped to get off at four this afternoon to go visit her grandparents. It didn't look like that would be happening.

"The wild one." Sandy rolled her eyes and slid the chart in front of Esther. "I can see if Dianne will take her, but you know the mood she's in today."

"No, that's fine." Esther took the chart from the med tech's hand. "I'll see her. Let's not ruffle Dianne's feathers if we don't have to."

Esther opened the chart as she stepped to the exam room door. Bailey Lewis was a frequent flyer and had developed a reputation for being hard to handle. Dianne, the other nurse practitioner, took turns seeing her and technically, today was Dianne's day. Dianne had already been vomited on first thing this morning, however, and Esther decided it would be better for the entire staff if she just saw the child instead.

A barking cough sounded on the other side of the door as Esther placed her hand on the handle. That didn't sound good. "Is there a puppy loose in here?" She stepped into the room and looked behind the trash can, then walked over and looked on the other side of the exam table. "I know I heard barking in here. Bailey Lewis, did you bring a puppy into this clinic?"

"No." Bailey's forehead wrinkled with a determine frown. "That was me and I'm not a dog."

"You?" Esther put her hands on her hips and looked down at the spunky little blond. She had obviously picked out her own attire this morning. Lime green sweatpants stuck out from under a flouncy red dress with puffy sleeves and a lacy collar. One leg of the sweats was tucked into her worn cowboy boots and the other was stretched around the top of it. "Are you sure you don't have a puppy under the tail of that pretty red dress?" She slipped her stethoscope from the pocket of her scrubs and inched closer to the child. Bailey Lewis was a kicker and it paid to move in slowly.

"I told you no." The child coughed again, and Esther looked over at Drake, sitting in the nearby chair. That was another reason she didn't mind seeing the tenacious child, the real reason, actually. Whenever the opportunity to look at Drake Lewis presented itself, Esther took it. She had known Drake, Quin and Hank ever since her parents had moved to Carson's Bayou when she was a kid in junior high. She'd had a crush on him almost as long.

"She's had a snotty nose for a few days, but that coughing, and the fever started last night." Drakes, deep somber voice filled the little exam room, and he stood up by the table where Bailey sat, stretching his large rough hands out on the white paper liner. "Since she gets the croup so easily, I figured I'd better bring her on in."

"You did the right thing." Esther put the stethoscope in her ears and leaned in closer. "Okay, Bailey, it's time for me to take a listen."

"No." Bailey's eyes shot daggers at Esther and she leaned over on Drake, away from Esther. "I don't like you and you're not touching me." She pulled her knee in and kicked out, but Esther swerved, dodging the strike.

"Alright, Bailey Paige." Drake eased his daughter up straight. "You remember what we talked about on the way here? If you cooperate, I'll get you a doughnut from the coffee shop when we're done. If you show out and act like you don't have any raisings, we're going straight home."

"Can I get a doughnut with chocolate on top and one

with pink on top?" Bailey cut her eyes up at her father and coughed again, right on cue.

Esther watched the child, amazed at how she played Drake Lewis, one of the toughest men in the parish, like he was a base fiddle. Back when they were in high school, Drake had been the captain of the football team and had often been involved in pranks played on rival schools. When she and Barlow had been away at college, Drake had gotten a reputation for being wild, drinking, and partying every weekend. Back then, Barlow or the rest of her conservative family would have let her go out with Drake Lewis, or any of the Lewis boys. Not that he had ever given her a second glance. He hadn't.

Then, ten years ago, when Esther had come home for Christmas break during her sophomore year of college, she liked to have fallen off her seat in the choir when Paige Floyd came walking through the back doors of the church with Drake on her arm. Before she went back to school two weeks later, Drake had given his life to Christ. She had gone back to college and the next thing she heard, the two had gotten married and Drake's wild partying ways had come to a stop.

"Yes, I'll get you whatever you want. Just let Miss Esther listen to your chest." Drake looked down at his daughter, his eyebrows raised. "Do we have a deal?"

"I'll do it," the little girl said, poking her lips out, "but I still don't like her and I think she's fat and ugly too."

Read Kid Smarts and Wistful Hearts

Sign up for KC's newsletter to receive a free eBook of Music Smarts and Humble Hearts

A Christmas Blaze

Fresh Starts and Small Town Hearts

Business Smarts and Reckless Hearts

Car Smarts and Bashful Hearts

People Smarts and Wounded Hearts

Kid Smarts and Wistful Hearts

Family Smarts and Runaway Hearts

Elsie: Prairie Roses Collection

Moonlight, Murder and Small Town Secrets

Music, Murder and Small Town Romance

Memories. Murder and Small Town Money

Merry Murder and Small Town Santas

Medicine Murder and Small Town Scandal

Marriage, Murder & Small Town Schemes

Mistaken Murder & Small Town Status

Mistletoe, Murder & Small Town Scoundrels

Join KC's Newsletter to receive an eBook copy of Music Smarts and Humble Hearts

ACKNOWLEDGMENTS

Thank you to my Savior for giving me this story. Callie and her rebellious streak hit a little too close to home for my comfort. In the end, as a child of a wonderful and gracious God, he has never forsaken me, his underserving child and blessed me beyond measure.

Thank you to my wonderful readers who supported me through my dry spell this year where, for many boring reasons, I was unable to finish this story. It is finally here for you to enjoy.

As with every book, thank you Mr. Wonderful for your loving support.

A LITTLE ABOUT KC

KC Hart is the author of best-selling Christian cozy mysteries, contemporary inspirational small-town romance, and has also dabbled in historical romance as well. KC is an independent publisher and released her first title, book one of the Katy Cross cozy mystery series, the summer of 2020. KC's goal is to seamlessly bring entertaining stories full of small-town life to her readers that gently weave in the faith and the love of Christ.

KC lives in rural Mississippi with Mr. Wonderful, her husband of thirty-nine years. When she is not writing, she is playing her piano or guitar, reading, or spending time with her family, especially the grandkids.

All KC's books are free of foul language, sex and graphic gore. KC says you can leave her books on the coffee table when your momma or the preacher stops in for a visit and you won't have to blush.

KC asks that you pray for her as she crafts new stories. Her desire is that each story will point the reader to Christ.

If you enjoyed this book, please take a few minutes to leave a review now. Authors, myself included, really appreciate this, and it helps draw more readers to books they may enjoy as well. Thanks! KC

Join KC's newsletter and receive a free ebook of Music Smarts and Humble Hearts

Follow KC on her social media platforms

https://www.goodreads.com/author/show/20570083.K_C_Hart

https://www.bookbub.com/profile/kc-hart?list=author_books

www.amazon.com/author/kchartauthor

https://www.facebook.com/KCWRITESBOOKS

www.ingramcontent.com/pod-product-compliance
Lightning Source LLC
Chambersburg PA
CBHW020839260626
47169CB00003B/1058